T0110327

CACTUS
BLOOM

CACTUS BLOOM

(Collection of Songs, Poems, Short Stories, Excerpts, and a One-Act Play)

Binai Chandra Rai

PARTRIDGE
A Penguin Random House Company

Copyright © 2014 by Binai Chandra Rai.

ISBN: Softcover   978-1-4828-1644-0
             Ebook   978-1-4828-1645-7

All rights reserved. No part of this book may be used or reproduced by any means, graphic, electronic, or mechanical, including photocopying, recording, taping or by any information storage retrieval system without the written permission of the publisher except in the case of brief quotations embodied in critical articles and reviews.

Because of the dynamic nature of the Internet, any web addresses or links contained in this book may have changed since publication and may no longer be valid. The views expressed in this work are solely those of the author and do not necessarily reflect the views of the publisher, and the publisher hereby disclaims any responsibility for them.

To order additional copies of this book, contact
Partridge India
000 800 10062 62
www.partridgepublishing.com/india
orders.india@partridgepublishing.com

CONTENTS

OF DESIRES

CONTEMPLATION

EXPRESSIONS

OF LOVE AND HATE

DEDICATIONS

SHORT STORIES, ARTICLES, ONE-ACT PLAY

There's a lonely road ahead
I know I have to make it on
my own
Doesn't matter if I'm scared,
or if I'm petrified . . . .
Until I take my last step
Until it's travelled and it's
done
The isolation all along can't
be denied . . . .

So take me away, into a
crowd not as a stranger
Place me with someone
unknown and let there be,
Conversation . . . .

To my grandparents (RIP) for the Wisdom and Stories;

To *Pop* and *Maa* for their unconditional love and everything;

To *Bada* and *Badi* for the guidance and strength;

To my *Aunt* for the care and understanding;

To my best friends for always being there (you know who you are);

To my in-laws for the support and companionship;

And to my wife for believing in me more than myself and egging me to keep going . . . .

SONNET

FROM CRIES IN SAP

3rd June '02

The unevenness of your dual shade
Have you your sun to keep away the fade?
As the dark granules, could make you jaded
Before the pure rain, is reinstated.
The vibe of eagerness to shed their bloom
If be the metals, far from spelling doom.
And when they seem silent, you hear their cries
You wish for a mind like your mouth and eyes.
The viscous tears reflects a cry for some
As they see the suffocation to come.
And its bare stance in autumn, just for lives
Is the time, for genuine care that it strives.
But when instead they fall in stillness trap
Graven images are from cries in sap.

AFTERGLOW

24th Feb '07

The serenity of darkness has spread
Across the azure revealing the sparkles,
Biggest and closest; one that most startles,
Hiding and appearing; own pace instead.
The ashen puffs flow by as if wanting,
To wipe off, of your seraphic wholesome.
Even the peaceful mind finds troublesome,
She whispers, 'Leave it to the revolving.'
Like the night torch she sends showers of white
All who bathe in them write, sing, see; spellbound
Tranquil face of our blazing you reflect . . . .
Faithful to the soil, you circle your light
Us; even hypnotized, if you had sound
In your afterglow if be, I'd accept . . . .

SERIES OF
CRIES

WITH RESPECT TO

17th Feb '00

Wonder how this mind doesn't get bored
Even after thinking about that tiresome graduation
No matter how far it may seem
It still wants to strive on the execution of elevation

Maybe,
    Deep inside it knows, there's still a child being born
    No doubt they keep vanishing, but still there's a child being born

When you start thinking relatively
You'll never find yourself down and ugly
And if being below troubles you
Just think you're surely above a few

Because there's always the zero level
And so much for the fable
Stay calm and latch on to your dream cable

Maybe, someday,
Deep inside you'll know, there's still a
child being born
No doubt they keep vanishing, but still
there's a child being born . . . .

NUMB

3rd Mar '00

Your truth goes un-believed
When you're on a high profile
And the only way to put them through
Is you have to step out of style

And when you meet a lot for a day
And think that there's more to come
Somewhere inside the impact starts to fade
And all you feel is sort of numb

There're so many anxious hearts around
There's so much love you have to give
But the sadness comes in as the sun goes
down
The feeling within gets the touch of short live

And on top of it,
    When you get touched a lot for a day
    And think that there's more touch to come
    Somewhere inside the feeling starts to
disappear
    And all you feel is sort of numb

And if the question comes along alone
I can't help it, I just can't
Since all I can do is keep going,
Keep trying, as there's no de-numb chant;
In my head, for my head, for my heart
That's already started on the numb from within
That's already started on the numb from within

Until, I hope when I can do, with numb without
Until, I can do, with numb without
Until I feel fine, with numb gone out.

THERE . . . .

14th Mar '00

There lies a broken tomb
Did a soul escape?
Its RIP bound in dust
Into the unknown shape

There hides a broken heart
Did the feelings run away?
To return at times to tease
Leaving the state of desperate pray

Desperate pray;
For that span void of love
To leave, to return, again
And this time taking along
To save all from the extra pain

There ends the straight path
Did it reveal what's round the bend?
If it's the same or not,
Or a time to pretend

There's the closing going on
Did it bring that killer instinct?
Extracting each and every element
And getting them inter-linked

Inter-linked;
    To create a phenomenon
    In a manner extraordinary
    Like once a long time ago
    Immortal, even if not physically

GO ON

28th Mar '00

There's the sky up there
That makes the climb in front insignificant
And among many who ponder
Some might call me an insane infant

But if this thought had a voice
And this mind the ability to explain
Maybe every head would have made that choice
And accepted the turning act as fun and sane

I just wanted to visualize;
    My goal in the sky
    And the path in the climb
I just wanted to realize;
    How hard I have to try
    In the slowly slipping time

So whenever a head turns up
I will not be the one to scorn
I would rather put on a smile
And speak in silence, 'Go On, Turn On.'

MOCK ADOPTION

23rd Aug '00

A change had come long before
To tell how, the reason I never had
A long term fever ended for sure
To the relief, there was nothing more to add

It was like time had turned its face to another
mirror
Without any thought for my then resolution
Now being ahead, when I match my head
back in time
I was with myself in mock adoption

Right now, a change is sneaking in
Holding no grudge against the outward
assistance
When I myself decided
To reduce my effort of resistance

And it feels bad, on turning your face away
from someone you love
Like an act of ironic substitution
And when again the silence is broken and
smiles restored
I find myself in total mock adoption

UNWANTED

9th Sep '00

There is a fire burning
But it flickers
As the wind is blowing
Among our strangers

And as the mouth opens
They slowly begin to lose
Their grips to those words
Only desperation to choose

Well, I feel I'm slowly being one of them
When I know, I should be holding on
    Ready in all for the unexpected
    Ready to face the power of the unwanted

It sure is tough
To raise those fallen heads
When hope is fading fast
Among our living deads

And even as they rise
It's the same faces again
Now, void of any smile
Taken by that virtual pain

Well, I feel my face slipping out of my will
When I know, I should be smiling on
    Ready in all for the unexpected
    Ready to face the power of the unwanted

HARD TO DIGEST

10th Sep '00

Some innocent bones get crushed
So many hearts get rushed
So many minds arrive
Into frozen land, still alive

When her life was about to show
Its new phase in complete glow
Just for some mindless driver
She struggles to be a survivor

If they make it, the idols are in fame
It they don't, the same may be in shame

And when I think of it,
Over and over again; I cannot get any rest
Since it's so much, too much,
And too hard to digest

So, I re-lit the candlestick
Hoping to undo the dog's cry
Might sound a bit crazy
But it may be worth a try

Since it's so hard to digest; so much, too
much . . . .
Too hard to digest . . . .

FIGHTING HER TIME

9th Jan '01

There are fruits by the leaves
On an artistic conglomeration
When the magic hot sips
Makes you rise to the frequency modulation

Then you're back to senses
Consciousness stretching its way
Through all those pretenses
Fading, fast, day by day

While the green drive ways changing
To the damned exhalation
So many sights are in endless spinning
From the spontaneous inflammation

And when you come out of the temporary
ecstasy
Onto your feet, to meet the natural fantasy
You cannot find, you cannot find
The end to this state of mime
And when the focus shifts
You see that she's just, fighting her time

You see that she's been praying
For millions of misses
Despite the hurt and overburdening
For her children she wishes

And when the subset goes along
Unnoticed, coming back again
It's the same fruits by the leaves
Ripe and hard to restrain

And when you come out of the temporary
ecstasy
Onto your feet, to meet the natural fantasy
You cannot find, you cannot find
The end to this state of mime
And when the focus shifts
You see that she's just, fighting her time

WEB OF HATE

13th Oct '01

Close your eyes
Since it's getting dark outside
Not that there's any
Black hole in sight
It's the cultivated disease called insecurity

Block your ears and mind
To the silence that is growing
Not because,
The evening is fast arriving
It's because the land is charred, by their
wars

And you will never know
If there will be another dawn
To tear this web of hate
You never know
If there will be another call
To tear this web of hate
And you never know
If there will be a new day
Without this web of hate

ROUGH ON FLESH

28ᵗʰ Oct '01

Still new tears
For patches sewn
All his dears
Unknown misty fume

    The tender palms
    Mostly facing heaven
    For shiny charms
    Being hunger driven

And how long before
His feet retreats into warmth's recess
And how long to go
Before there's no more rough on flesh, no
more rough on flesh . . . .

On the floor
Immune to touch
The hidden sore
Of killing clutch

    And even though
    Wanting to fly
    'I don't know'
    Cried her eyes

And how long before
Her soul is invited into love's recess
And how long to go
Before there's no more rough on flesh, no
more rough on flesh . . . .

A DAY, THAT'S NEVER YESTERDAY

6th Nov '01

Shivers run along
When I think
About the sunken heavyweight
It gets cold in rage
When I think
About the lives it ate

Why couldn't it have been?
Like a part of fiction; framed
Since I do not need
Yet another date, to be named
For the cries I couldn't hear
Trapped and engulfed with fear

And I do not need
Yet another day; A day,
That's never yesterday . . . .

BE MY CHAMELEON

23rd Nov '01

If this upside down
Was true with gills and fins
I'd wink, fate,
To by my cuttlefish

If there was a way
To undo you from oblivion
I'd beg, fate,
To be my chameleon

If by means of any slit
I could sneak to be Orpheus
I'd paralyze my neck
For the sake of all of us

And if there was a way
To undo you from oblivion
I'd beg, fate,
To be my chameleon

If I could be the one
To use the walnut and *makhamali*
I'd plead, fate,
To be my fantasy

And would it then be easy
To undo you from oblivion
Would then I have to beg
Fate to be my chameleon?

SO FAR SINCE

5th Dec '01

Every time you break your skin
The ecstasy keeps growing thin
And with each and every pinch
You are like, so far since . . . .

You knew that all it took
Was just to breathe
And now, when you look
You need aid, just to breathe

And with each and every pinch
You are like, so far since
The first wrong step you took
As you reflect, as you look

You're so called heaven
Can never be bought nor sold
So your favorite cloud
Is never going to hold
As soon, after that pinch
When you feel the cold

You realize with each and every pinch
You've come, so far since

THE DARK, THE WHITE, THE WISE

6th Mar '02

Each new day I get along
I have to fake having a good time
Laughing around in every word
Making things appear sublime

I feel I've left
A whole part of me back where I belonged;
In the form of the dark, the white and the wise . . . .

Each day I set for a song
I get stuck so many times
Notes getting hard to handle
Even though I get to the rhymes

And I fell I'm waiting
For a whole part of me, here, where I belong;
In the form of the dark, the white and the wise
In the form of the dark, the white and the wise

AUTUMN OF MY MIND

9th Mar '02

Well I don't know
What's wrong in me
Of all the new things
Coming for free
The one that spills
The spark of doubt
Has got me
To think about
    All those times
    Through which we died
    Now just seems
    So sucked up and dried

And I feel it's the autumn of my mind

Well when you came
Back on line again
All those talks
Felt so in vain
And the one that adds
The touch of pain
Had got me
To think again
    About the times
    Through which we cried
    Now just seems

So sucked up and dried
Through which we died
Not just seems
So sucked up and dried

And I feel it's the autumn of my mind
It's the autumn of my mind

THE ELLIPSOIDAL HARMONY

20th Apr '02

Like shackles to the sea
And they were free
Why not guns to the ground
And peace be found

Since it's not our fault
That we were born under diversity
So why make it worse
By killing what's meant to be, the ellipsoidal
harmony

Wars are all the same
They have always destroyed
And what be of the victory
When all that'll remain is void

And it's not our fault
That we were born under diversity
So let's not make it worse
By killing what's meant to be, the ellipsoidal
harmony

DESTRUCTION OF PARADISE

25th May '02

The day the clouds form the wall
Would it matter, if you stood tall?
Beneath the blanket of your deed
As insanity exceeds,
    The power to lure
    Of your conscience; pure

Then, no tears I would say
Please, don't cry, I would say
Albeit pity is close, it's not for you
It's meant for the suffering true

    So, no tears, I say
    And don't cry, I say
    As the sight of emotion
    Rolling down your eyes
    Gives a vision
    Of destruction of paradise

When things get hard to be seen
Will we get to see the color green?
Amidst the barren haze of gold and dry
In the sun's final try,
    To shatter the sheet
    And make feel its heat

Still no tears, I would say
And don't you cry, I would say
As the least you want is thirst to call
In the day the clouds, gives up its wall

So, no tears, I say
And don't cry, I say
As the sight of pain
Rolling down your eyes
Enhance the vision
Of destruction of paradise

BEAMED INTO OMISSION

3rd Feb '03

When I caught sight of near perfection
I entered into a state of omission
From all the pretentious faces there was
Gaping and freezing, left, I was

Like from nowhere it had beamed
Superficial, then it seemed
As it was robbed from its right to dance
With recovery, never as a chance

You should've rooted
Their brains more than needed
You should've made them kneel
More than they pleaded
You should've barked
That they're taking more than enough
You should've told what they did
Was more than enough

INCOGNITO

SWAYING BRAIN

23rd March '98

The pacer ate me up
I lost my shivering faith
I felt I failed a test
As only less went in as breath

Sure something's awkward,
I feel I'm out of track
In the stream of my swaying thoughts,
With baseless belief in stack

Something is awkward,
I do feel something's not sane
Since the thoughts are of my mind,
And the mind is of the brain
My brain is swaying, and me,
I'm asking a swaying brain . . . .

DEVILISH GOD

8th April '98

Would anyone believe; the devil turned into a god.
Though it still looked the same—red, arrow-tipped tail with pointed ears?

Would anyone love; that god of a devilish look?

If the answer turns out to be a 'Yes', then it would sound hard to accept.
When all seems to be taken in, by the appearance concept.

Where change has to struggle for acceptance, even if it is for the better.
Where perception is controlled, by the first impression fever.

TRAPPED INVINSIBILITY

9th Sep '98

Deep inside I feel that I'm so lonely,
Lonely as a barren land
But my mind keeps on saying, that this
loneliness is just a thought . . . .
So then I think for a while
Having everything within me
I might have found the answer, I have long
sought . . . .

    That deep down inside, I know
    Though it's strange to know
    That within a mortal hierarchy
    Dwells the deathless eternity . . . .

So, again I think for a while
Why we feel the pain
To the infliction caused by practical
abilities . . . .
And deep inside I feel
A surge of vulnerability
And I'm exposed to questions, in all
possibilities . . . .

That deep down inside, do I know?
Is it strange to know?
That within a mortal hierarchy
Dwells a questionable eternity . . . . ?

Seems that though indestructible
The soul may still be susceptible
To the virtual weapons and arms
That diffuses causing no physical harms
Till it reached deep down inside
Where it causes all the fright . . . .

INSIDE YOUR UNKNOWN CONTRADICTIONS

9th Aug '01

When people told to be made for each other
Doesn't shed their jealous robe of silent war
You begin to think; how do they talk about
intimacy

When the ones who made promises to one
another
Doesn't shed their ego; try till they win
You cannot understand, how they claim
loyalty

And could it be for real?
And is it so; love faded with time
Succumbing to mortal intentions
And could it be for sure?
And is it so, you got caught
Inside your unknown contradictions

NEMESIS

11th Oct '01

Don't feel strange,
If you wish for intelligent airplanes
As there's a fool on the run
Don't be ashamed,
If you wish for elastic frames
There are fools following the gun

And if you ever cry
For infants with leaded lullaby
Be glad you can still show your face
Since for the fools, that's not the case

For the fool on the run
For the fools following the way of the gun
Blinded by their insane blitz
They are headed towards their nemesis

OF DESIRES

COINCIDE

8th July '98

All set to be somewhere else
But somehow ended up at the same place
Because my ears had to receive
That too at the time of leave

Isn't it a great incidence?
Or just a coincidence . . . .

Next was that innocence
Becomes the cause of incense
And the cause of anger and insanity
Is one who has no fault of any

Isn't it a strange incidence?
Or just a coincidence . . . . ,
A great incident? A strange incident? A
coincidental incident . . . .

So, if it was to coincide:
 Hope love and mind coincide
 Consciousness being forever by their side
 Hope knowledge and death coincide
 No grief of the end to hide
 Hope dream and dedication coincide
 So every dream's a reality bona fide
 Let soul and purity coincide
 To rebirth none had to abide
 Let this wish and the decision coincide
 To initiate the removal of the plight . . . .

UNTITLED

26th May '99

If I ever could
I would have painted this world all blue and
green
If I ever had a wish
I would have had the Pandora's Box never
to be seen

If there was a way
I would have paved it with all possible
solutions
If there was a hope
I would have made it appear at all conditions

If only I could
And that's only if I could
There would be nothing I wouldn't have done
To restore peace and love under the same
sun . . . .

ALL IN A WISH—I

10th Aug '99

Wish I was buried alive
And made born dead
So I could take an eternal dive
Into silent peace without being afraid

Wish I was made perfect
If I had to live
Senseless in all respect
With nothing but sanity to give

But you have to take
And still you have to think
Not sure if you have to fake
But you just cannot live for a blink

You wish to be mistake free
Wish to be what you want to be
You wish your wishes remained wishes no
more
No more remaining as dreams like they were
before

OK, BUT IF . . . .

22nd Nov '99

All I want is some time of my own
To get a little bit of some free air
All I wish is such a world to exist
Where eternity always comes with pair

These grains would've been just fine
If there weren't any pre-fixed scripts

All I want is a head as cool as ice
That would work as soon as the heat is on
All I wish if for such a thinking tank
That would catch those needed times before
they're gone

This entangled jelly would've been just great
If it weren't troubled to hell at times

All I want is a heart that's so, so pure
Even intentionally unable to desire wrong
All I wish is for such a bag of feelings
That's nice and soft and at the same time
strong

This pumping flesh would've been just the
one needed
If it weren't so susceptible and evil at times

And 'all I want' is just an irony
Since it's never ever going to be 'All'
As you won't be able to say, just,
When your desires start to fall

ALL IN A WISH—II

4th Jan '00

Wish I could just get into a chamber
And come out as a lunatic
Making wonders, engraved with my mind
Those are more than just fantastic
Wish I was a maniac
Who could solve them all the way
Or a hell of a creator
Who could make a world good enough to stay
Upon which the first blaze
Brings nothing but the wanted peaceful day

WISH ALL PRECEDES

20th Feb '00

When the first feeling of existence,
Comes in with a grip over your chest,
You know you will have a painful transition.
When the end of several decades to breath,
Comes in a flash before your eyes,
You know you will have a choking sensation.

So you wish that all precedes
So you could pile up the left-over agonies
Such that the choking sensation, slowly,
    Becomes choking no more . . . .
The painful transition, soothingly,
    Becomes no more a sore . . . .

When you think about the pain to cares you
give.
You wish relationships didn't exist at all.
But as these binding bonds are bound tight
You wish all precedes before your fall
You wish all precedes before your fall . . . .

THE BLISS

19th Mar '00

It isn't the way it should
Knowing that your lines are good
When there are things to be done
And you can't push yourself against the sun

The phrases that were told
Becomes just another fold
And your days run so fast
From your side into the past

Then you find yourself
Making that helpless wish
Then you tire yourself
Searching that wanted bliss

And don't find it strange
Seeing that the lines has changed
Because things were left undone
When you gave yourself to the sun

And the phrases that were told
Becomes just another fold
And as your day turns into night
In the remaining light;
Yes, in the remaining light . . . .

You find yourself . . . .

Then you find yourself
Releasing that helpless wish
Rejuvenating yourself
In the light of internal bliss

THE FLOAT

19th Aug '01

Someday, somewhere, sometime
I hope to be in the float within
Of modest intentions
And deeds that will be seen
Where everybody thinks, there, they are alone
Time as such defined; to full dilation, it has
grown

Then don't remind me of pacification
If I am flying to high
Because I know I'll reach justification
As time goes by . . . .

(SHOUT-SCREAM)

12th June '02

I'm in need of a time machine
For my search of the killer of sin
And as there are none to be seen
How about a hand, to save our skin?

(Shout-Scream)

I'm in need of the power to raven
The mushrooms that cannot be eaten
And as they are just dust and no fun
How about your head for right things to be
done?

(Shout-Scream)

I'm in need of the power to blow
For you to see the sky in its glow
But as the passion begins to go
How about some words to make is slow

(Shout-Scream)

I'm in need of some days gone by
To undo, patch, color and deny
The source that caused many to lie
But time keeps flowing; I still don't know why

(Shout-Scream)

COME OFF THE PLEAD

2nd Dec '02

Though I'm way past, a quarter of my life
I feel I was just born yesterday
When a smile on one of thousands
Helped me find my way

Through the complications
That seemed impenetrable
Through the formulations
For questions unanswerable

And what I needed was not the oasis
But the sand as my sheath
What I needed was not the shade
But to feel the heat
And to come off the plead

Though I may be way past my head
I'm sane enough to say
That a virus is better
In an amazing kind of way

It doesn't know
Any discrimination
It doesn't care
Of any identification

So what we need is not the oasis
But the sand as our sheath
What we need is not the shade
But to feel the heat
And come off our plead

CONTEMPLATION

THE DROP, THE EXPANSION, THE BURST

22nd Sep '97

Where does the air come from?
　　There isn't any below.
Must have been sent from the unseen,
　　So even in the dark, it may glow.
Where does the air go from?
　　Sure there isn't any hole.
Might have got frustrated enough,
　　And decided to go away with the soul.
How does the air go from?
　　Haven't yet traced its trace.
Wherever it goes, however it goes,
　　Only a few must have made it to the space.
Why does the air go from?
　　Trapped, it shouldn't have felt nor feel.
Might have felt closed in a transparency of see but not do,
　　Hence, flew away in search for the heal.

Where, How, Why, the air came and went
from?
How, Why, Where, the air went and came
from?
    Where would the answer come from?
    Where would the voice sound from?
    Telling me not to hasten,
    And how and when would my mind listen?

Because all I see is,
    The Drop, The Expansion, The Burst
Because my attempts to understand,
    Tires out somewhere in the crust
And at the end it's still,
    The Drop, The Expansion, and The Burst.

Where does the air come from?
    There isn't any below.
Was it sent from the unseen?
    Since even in the dark, it doesn't glow.

But I still see,
    The Drop, The Expansion, The Burst
My attempts to understand,
    Still tires out somewhere in the crust
And at the end it's still,
    The Drop, The Expansion, and The
Burst . . . .

ULTIMATE TAKEOVER

10th Oct '97

Sluggish or a Flick?
 It's sometimes slow
 Other times hardly a sudden
 Till the red is washed and the white dome
turned
 Don't sprout the wish to be forgiven

Patient or Hasty?
 It takes the goods away
 Sometimes late, sometimes too soon
 The ultimate is of the root
 Like the night belonging to the moon

Yes! I did come
To feed the greatest hangover
Closer of the gap
The ultimate takeover

Going down to it . . . .
All going down to it!
Then going up with it . . . .
All going up with it!

I

'97—early '98

Sometimes I fell, that it's only a dream
Then I come to know, that I wasn't asleep.
I often glare, at the white glittered black
Someday I'll be there, then looking back.
At the sphere where, I'll have to come
Being caught in the loop, hope it's just some.
As I don't want to rebound,
Due to the faults that I've done
I want to diffuse,
For which I'm a real stubborn

    And this is filled with 'I'
    This I cannot lie
    Since I'm in search of a life
    That's free from disguise . . . .

The belief's fading away,
From me of the mind of my own
How quickly the seed got rot,
That for such a long time I'd sown
And I cannot say it's wrong,
As my heart isn't feeling bad
Neither can I say it is right,
Since if the had wasn't 'is', I'd have been glad
I do want to proceed, but the past is still a
spreaded sheet

And the fear too remains, that in the future,
the same may repeat . . . .

And what I found hidden,
Was what I see behind a mirror . . . .
Of a state of my mind
Taken in by confusion and horror . . . .

    And this is still about 'I'
    And this I cannot lie
    Hope it's a smile instead of sigh
    Hope it's not a crash, but a high fly
    Hope it's a solution, which I can apply
    Since I'm in search of a life, that's free
from disguise . . . .

TESTED TO HELL

9th May '98

Stuck in a place which I know, yet know not what
Feel like a bunch of obstacles, on the start
Near the verge of breakdown, living with option lack
A small piece of life, treading on the right track

Evacuation bringing up the urge
To look at that hands on the lurch
The urge then bringing about the drive
The settling drive, never wanting to strive

You meet your flying friends, when you go for a throw
The splashes comes back, when you make the hot river flow
On losing your weight, you have to deal in the dark
When in need, even what's enough is just a spark

Just like a feather in a sway
Fine and fit in every way
Waiting for the moment to settle down
To go high again after hitting the ground

Bounding your wishes isn't that easy
Fighting your sources makes you crazy
Stopping is tough of making giving up a
habit
But when you have to get down with it, you
are down with it . . . .

TURNOVER

10th Feb '00

I would rather see a stray dog, than turn my
head to a worshipped idol
Think on its situation, than in my mind, let
those lines fiddle

Because it's enough living on 'Why', without
its 'It's like this'
Because now it's enough of the maze play,
and its pin-hole like bliss

However, I will not miss the pleasure of
praying
For that I will create my own gods
Until, yes, when prayers become absolute
I can simply pray, without the need of any
gods

Who would like to continue with the question
(Q)?
With an expected reciprocation denied
With more of a one-way traffic then two
With most of the answers lying beside

There should have been equal rounds of As
and Qs
There should have been transparent
explanations, instead of the virtual excuse

However, I will not miss the joy of wondering
For that I will cultivate my head
Until, yes, the time goes by its last flick
And I go into slumber on my darkness
bed . . . .

FINE LINE

24th Mar '00

I want to breathe, as far and deep as I can
To feel life diffuse, in each and every drop of
blood of mine
I want to open wide, with a filter of course
In my eyes and mind, to be able to see that
fine line

Yes, that fine line;
    Between life and death
    Between hate and faith
    Between thick and thin
    Between deed and sin

So many faces and instant in change
In a second you're without, with and without
So I want to meditate and do every crazy thing
To make a stand and not to shout

So for you I can shine
Understanding that fine line

Yes, that fine line;
    Between a break and a fix
    Between all to all and a nix
    Between want and the satiated state
    Between belief and fate

ANGER PLAY

7th Mar '00

It's almost empty; only some left
You find the flaw as it's not done right
And when the source itself is in debt
How could she turn it into a delight

Then, sparks off the heat
Bringing out that slicing say
That goes through the fleshy sheet
Rest being history of the anger play

But here, there's no exchange,
Of verbal disarray
As only one is entitled
To cast its anger play

It simply slips out of hand
And you are still left unknown
Understanding just doesn't stand
Only the ignorance being shown

Then the spark off of heat is the same
Bringing out that love ridden say
That goes through the boney frame
Rest being history of the anger play

But here, there is an exchange
Of more than verbal disarray
As both are entitled now
To cast their anger play, to cast their anger
play
Being more than just an anger play . . . .

CURIOUS MIND

20th June '00

Would I know when I would die, if I live a day
ahead?
Or would I have one more day, if I lived a
day behind instead?

(What can I do; I've got this curious mind!)

Wanting to know, what the young ones had
Against you oh seeked; that they ended so
bad

Would I be able to know, if I said those
words a zillion times?
If I could even live my life, without being a
victim to your crimes

(And I've got this curious mind!)

Wanting to know, how far had they seen
Before feeling the effect, of the reversal of
green . . . .

THE WALK

15th Sep '00

You don't feel bad
When pigments get killed
Your unconscious act
Keeps you thrilled

And after the pluck, comes the thought
So many wastes, just in the walk . . . .

A swing of leg
No harm is there
It's dry and brown
Far from the flare

And after the crush, there's the talk
So cheap and loud, just in the walk . . . .

'Me first' goes on
Till you open the lock
Then one finally wins
And the other's in mock

And after the race, comes the stalk
So many kill, just after the walk . . . .

CONJUGATE FACTORS

26th Dec '00

Sitting all alone
I'm trying to define
As what was shown
Was far from being fine
In this relation pool
At least, you have to stick
Even though you feel like a fool
Not able to hold that brick

Yes! I can't hold that brick
That's about as old as me
And it's making me sick
As it slips away into the sea

So, for any expectations, I'm not the Pied Piper
Even if I was one, cannot find an empty river
Since I'm not the only one, I'm not the only one
Who is living with those conjugate factors . . . .

LIFT

3rd Jan '03

Hey outside young marrows
Lift yourselves from that dirty old sink
There is no fountain of youth
Only your power with which to think

For a right choice from the wrong
A noise, from a song

Among many things that will not wait
Is the time you spend wearing that gaze
With a squat and a smoke
Drowned in your fuzzy craze

Wake up and smell the air
It's missing your essence
Wake up and be aware
It's missing your presence

To make right from the wrong
To know noise from a song

SEEK

'11—'12

You keep walking down the road
Never knowing where it will lead you to
Holding on to something that is
Beyond the battle between false and true

When I ask you why, you say, you're
searching for answers . . . .

And I know the questions
Are like weeds in the garden of your mind
No matter how much you pluck
They grow back, making you to turn behind

Then I feel bad that I asked
As I see you ask me with your eyes
For a reply, a reason, an answer
And a request to be hypnotized

EXPRESSIONS

WORDS FOR THE MESS

26th May '96

Look well before you step
Remember, before you forget
Think twice, before you speak
Learn to accept, before you regret

Since outside, there's a big mess
Carved upon an ugly face
And you think who will succeed
In ploughing out the seed

If you ever try, to see deep inside
Do keep all the bad things aside
You better plan and prepare, before you
start
Listen to the beat of your heart

Since outside, there's a big mess
Carved upon an ugly face
And you think who will succeed
In ploughing out the seed

STRANGE

Nov '96

Wake up in the morning
Yet it's so dark
Hear the same cock crow
But now it sounds like an old dogs' bark

Nothing's the same as before
Everything's unusual, everything's bore
Can't see a solution for this sudden change
Since everything around, now seems to strange

Strange is the air
Strange is the water
Strange is the land
Strange is the lifestyle . . . .

The stars seem so close
Yet the sky is so far away
Who knows some of them might
Fall right upon us one day

Something's the same as before
So unusual and still a bore
Can't see a solution for this sudden change
Since everything around, now seems to strange

Strange is the air
Strange is the water
Strange is the land
Strange is the lifestyle . . . .

Past is all but remembrance
Present is all but now then never
Future is unknown yet so known
But the common thing is that they're all
strange

Strange is what happened
Strange is what's happening
Strange is what'll happen
Strange is the ongoing . . . .

MISTAKE

10th Sep '00

When the source of life flow in
Before the legal drama
There'll be a serious situation
Struggle with dharma and karma

So you better stick to your will
Fell safe in your patience lake
Instead of hastily closing your mind
Only to open to your foolish mistake

When the so called great minds
Make yet another history
Riding high on their bursting menace
I really do feel sorry

So stop making insecurity your alibi
Bring our home down from your stake
That's loaded with your useless fireworks
Standing as an epitome, of your fatal mistake

IN THE SPUN

14th Feb '01

An astronaut was asked, just minutes after
her escape
How our earth looked like
She said she sure is blue
Like she had seen her the first time
But now, traces of origin was on the low
She thought it could be just another show
Then she told him, if he were to be there
He sure would've felt
That the color of jealousy does indeed look
good, somewhere, down there

And what could he say
But just to stay
Knowing that he too was done,
    In the spun, in the spun

Sister was asked, just as they passed by a
graveyard
By a small boy of five, what those crosses were
She said with a smile on her face
That they show those who have gone
Somewhere far, and to say,
At night they can be seen as stars
But the sight of the tombs with whatever
sister had said

Brought an absence inside him that made
him ask again
Does it mean that now my mother is hiding
somewhere, down there?

And what could she pray
For his mind in gray
Knowing that he too wasn't spared, but done,
In the spun, in the spun

And the fact he knows
Sends shivers through her skin
Knowing the emptiness he feels
Just worsens the spin, just worsens the spin

A wise man was asked by his little son
On seeing his first heavy down pour
Dad, what's happening?
With tears in his eyes he said it's called
raining son
It's raining
Seeing tears in his father's eye
He then said
Are those dark clouds saying,
That our sky is in pain somewhere, up there?

BLIND TO AN ANGEL

14th Oct '01

She was the girl who saw
The black and white rainbow
When everyone there
Didn't care about her though

Since towards ignorance they were led
By the colors that tricked and bled

And failing over and over again
Finally, they did succeed
Being deaf and blind to an angel;
A sad and ghastly deed

She was the girl who showed
The sphere in red and gray
But everyone there
Didn't listen to what she had to say

Since to death they had made their call
Into darkness, they were to fall

And failing over and over again
Finally, they did succeed
Being deaf and blind to an angel;
A sad and ghastly deed

SHOE SHINE

2nd Nov '01

Shoe shine, shoe shine
Yes! Shoe shine
Anyone need a shoe shine?
Yes! A shoe shine
Come on, shoe shine

That dust doesn't look good on your feet
Give yourself a chance to treat
Come on, shoe shine

Come on, shoe shine
Let my brush dance on your leather
Let me help you get together
Yes! Shoe shine
Come on shoe shine

Shoe shine, shoe shine
Yes! Shoe shine
You need a shoe shine
Yes! A shoe shine
Come on, shoe shine

Come to your colors my man
Let me make you understand
The shoe shine; Yes! The shoe shine

Shoe shine, shoe shine
Oh Yes! The shoe shine
Shiny and fine
Yes! Shoe shine
Come on, shoe shine

IN WOMB

7th Nov '01

You don't need
To gasp for air
To feel the suffocation
When battles are there
To give you away
Its free invitation

Then you start to fret
However hard you concentrate

There's no use
In running around
To find that rotation
When battles are still there
To bring you back
In full restoration

Then you start to fret
No matter how hard you concentrate
And whatever care you take
You slip and they break

And you cannot run away
And you cannot avoid
No matter what care you take
You cannot speed away
You cannot avoid
You slip and their break

POST EXAMINATION FORMALITY

11th Nov '01

I get swept, by the thaw
Of the picture, I draw
Every time I'm in awe
Of my hand in flaw

Then all I can see
Is inside of the post examination formality

They got stuck, and slowed
When the figures rolled
Out the printed, and wrote
Like deduction overload

And don't ask, as you do see
Inside the post examination formality

EVAPORATE

14th Nov '01

It doesn't bleed
It never has
But you couldn't speak
If there was ash

And all it learnt
Was to erode
To see the burn
Fall on her abode

It hasn't bled
Someday, it might
Then you may shed
Tears just in spite

And all it learnt
Was to erode
To see the burn
Fall on her abode

And all I can keep
Is a clear slate
When the infinity within
Starts to evaporate

And all it learnt
Was to erode
To see the burn
Fall on her abode

AFTER FREEDOM

2nd Dec '01

Isn't is sad to hear
About the animal inside of us
Crossing the farthest line
Of savagery there ever was

Didn't you know
Innocence could be tricked and traded
So, why is she still
As an outcast still branded

And don't you know
She has come out of hell
Where her wishes doesn't count
And integrity's up for sell

So, what's holding you back?
To give her a little taste of heaven
Since from being a human
No one is forbidden, no one is forbidden

So, why are we holding back?
Give her, a little taste of heaven, a little
taste of heaven

RESOLUTIONS

1st Jan '02

Did he say?
He'd give up on those clouds
Coming out of him, laughing
How long before?
His will cries out loud
In the presence of its longing

Did he say?
He'd give up on the dark
Juicy brown tanner of the bones
And how long before
His mouth will ache and arch
In the absence of the drones

Did she say?
She'd give in to more touch
Of freshness to her senses
How long before?
She gives in as such
To her icy pretenses

Did she say?
She'd control on the thrill
Of her legs on the plain tar
And how long before
She's on the highway on pills
Slow to the lights so far

SOAR

2nd Jan '02

By flesh on plastic
He killed the ring
Winning over the click
Before it could sing,
    Verses of denial

And when he reached home,
    Indeed he had flown
    Into the unknown
    And managed to come out fine
    Managed to come out fine

By feet on ground
He won the race
Before he was bound
By the grace,
    Of one who's fragile

And when he reached home,
    Indeed he had flown
    Into the unknown
    And managed to come out fine
    Managed to come out fine

GASOLINE TIN

26th Feb '02

Hey gasoline tin
Where are you going?
This isn't the road
You used to be rolling
    In the rhythm of your solemn whistle

Hey gasoline tin
There's a number on you
That same one
That gets me through
    The last rhythm of the days tussle

Hey gasoline tin
You're being thrown
Among innocence
To be blown
    By their rhythm of hustle

Did they forget?
You were made to burn for good
Hey gasoline tin
Exactly the way it should
    In the rhythm of your solemn whistle . . . .

INITIATE

13th Apr '02

So you know how to shoot
And you know how to kill
Do you know how to smile?
Better learn to feel
Better learn to be what you really are
A shining star, a shining start

Don't you see?
Ammunitions have become common
Do something tough
Take the pen; fight your demon
Reach out and you'll find
There are still many hands
Not turned into fists
And ready to make a stand

And if you cannot find one
Initiate
Become the one
Initiate

Learn to be what you really are
Not a shooting star; but a shining star

Initiate, initiate, initiate . . . .

SMOKY LUST

8th Nov '02

I can kill you like you never existed
And still not have my time of trial
Since I'm the poison, lethal rated
Before me, you all stand fragile

You made a mistake, of making me
You made a mistake, of helping me

And now you'll see, I'll take you all
Down to my house of dust
As a consequence
Of your smoky lust

I can toss you like a minute particle
And shatter you, to shame the elementary
And you cannot be skeptical
When I say, I'm the power, I'm the energy

You made a mistake, of making me
You made a mistake, of helping me
You made a mistake, of making me
You made a mistake, of releasing me

And now you'll see, as I take you all
Down to my house of dust
As a consequence
Of your smoky lust

GROWING GREED

19th Nov '02

He finds it hard to believe, that life's his friend
When it set him up, a very strange trend
To put a smile for every punch it sends
Forcing him to adopt, the style of pretend
There does stand thousands of icons to see
up to
There's also the word exception, for everyone
in view
Then he knows, he cannot find
A breeze, or a wind, for his mind

　　So he turns his head up
　　And sees the clouds cleared up
　　And as they cruise by
　　He's left with envy for the sky

And he doesn't care of the growing greed
As it's meant for the end of the feed
Of many a things that he doesn't need
Apart from his want to heal and stop the bleed

Every day started with a good hot cup of tea
With the smile that only he could see
It was then that he let in number three
That murdered the two's harmony
There were thousands of broken hearts around
But this time he had broken one so sound
And he knows he cannot find
The word, the sorry, for her mind

So he holds his head down
And sees the land of the ones underground
Sees them asleep in their immune beds
Then feels the envy for the dead

And he doesn't care of the growing greed
As it's meant for the end of his deeds
Of many things he shouldn't have done
As good times had just begun

He went about, smashing every time machine
he saw
Because for him, they were the biggest flaw
They couldn't go back on their own
They would never go back on their own
He was too tired to search for the one who
could
Millions of different carvings as there stood
Couldn't close his eyes as he had lost his
sleep
And there she lied, far away from his reach

And he didn't care of the growing greed
It was all to back up his plead
For a bit or rewind, here and there
For abundance of love, everywhere

And he doesn't care of the growing greed
As it's meant for the end of the feed
Of many a things that he doesn't need
Apart from his want to heal and stop the
bleed

ONE MORE FACE

15th Dec '02

I see half bodies through the pane
But never their faces in any lane
It's bright, but not much to gain
Fear my speech will go in vain

So I sit quiet in this metal case
Just like any other face
Straight and out of place
Straight and out of place

I see a continuum in front of me
Can't figure out what it's meant to be
And with a halt I'm stuck on the knee
And I'm back among faces, I'd never see

So I sit quiet in this rolling case
Just like any other face
Straight and out of place
Straight and out of place
Dull, without a grace

As I don't know, if I should dare
Cannot decide; it's never really clear
So I sit quiet in this metal case
Just like any other face
Straight and out of place
Straight and out of place

SO CALLED ELECTED

19th Oct '04

Tell me about this:

A group of idiots, rattling on plasticine
Shaping it up based on their liking
Sowing ideas that they are faithful
As long as everyone else are fooled
Resulting in enlarged mid-sections
And sedentary top-sections

And what picture does this make?
Certainly not of a serene lake
So, tell me about it
What picture does this make?
Certainly of an art representing the fake
So, should I tell you about it?

Nothing for the wanted
Nothing for the wounded
Nothing for those who are left
Everything for those who commit the theft

Every day, every time
From words to the last dime

And what picture does this make?
Certainly not of a serene lake
    So, tell me about it
What picture does this make?
Certainly of an art representing the fake
So, should I tell you about it?

Of the new groups of idiots, rattling on our
plasticine?

SEEK THE REMEDY

5th Jan '07

I swim into the pool of my thoughts
Diving deeper every now and again
No air needed here and I can say
There is no particular pain
I come across my childhood smile
And my friends are but a haze
My strokes sweep images that speak
Seeking remedy to my present place

And it's not indecision
That clogs my verbal power
Complication was a constant companion
Withering any blooming flower
And the fear that I carry
Somehow kept telling me
To give her some space
To seek the remedy for my present place

Reflection in flesh and blood, so fair
Talking to yourself becomes a reality
No confirmation needed here, for me to know
The delicate play of balance and serenity

Intoxication of a different kind
And my barricades are but ablaze
Crumbling to ashes to let her in
Maybe, she'll find remedy to her present place

And it's not indecision
That clogs my cerebral power
Complication was a constant companion
Withering any blooming flower
And the fear that I carry
Somehow kept telling me
To give her some space
To seek the remedy for her present place

INTRICATE PLAYGROUND

'07

This was where I used to be
Happy and so free
Simple things, we used to play
Marbles, goals, and break away

Now it's changed into a maze
Walls and dark days
Glimmer of hope? Mistaken
It's their mind play awaken

In their intricate playground
Of puppets without a sound
Glimmer of hope? Mistaken
It's their mind play awaken

Peace was here, it used to be
All around, naturally
In simple things, we used to know
Wind, stars and in the river flow

Now all has become, stories we share
Again and again, among our stares
Hint of reality? Forsaken
It's their mind play, awaken

In their intricate playground
Of puppets without a sound
Hint of reality? Forsaken
It's their mind play, awaken

CHILD IN ME

'08

I remember the days
When I used to see
The measure of life
Flowing out of me
When I used to sing
The song of time
That had no reason
Nor any rhyme

And whenever I felt
I was losing it all
I caught hold of the child in me
To prevent the fall

I realize nowadays
That I'm still alive
Going day after day
For my dreams, I survive
And I still do sing
A new song of now
Like just coming to me
Not knowing how

And when I feel
I'm losing it all
I'll catch the child in me
To prevent the fall

WASTED TIME

'10

Been around the world on a twenty four hour
Scheme of a lifetime trip
Had to think about a lot, but it was a chance
That I just didn't want it to slip

Went here to there and everywhere
Couldn't figure out what there was
Just went with the flow as I didn't want
To turn it into a terrible fuss

And I see it coming down on me
And I feel it slipping inside of me
That it was all, wasted time

Did lot of eating, did a lot of sleeping
Did a lot of drinking and got drunk
Wouldn't have a clue if the liner I was in
Went Titanic and sunk

So many faces to remember
Most of whom I forgot
The only thing retaining my sanity
Was that last tequila shot

And I see it coming down on me
And I feel it slipping inside of me
That it was all, wasted time

OF LOVE AND HATE

WONDERFUL TOUCH

23rd June '99

Feeling lonely is what I've done, for a long,
long time
Living with this mind executing, the
unstoppable crime
But now I think, it's my turn to come out
To feel at the top, and definitely shout

Because you just cannot whisper
Or you just cannot talk
When you get that wonderful touch
That even makes your numb part walk

Life was in its deepest blues
With all of mine for me to lose
Until it just happened, my mind got a mind
After which to the darkness, I was but a blind

Because you just cannot peep
Or you just cannot see either
When you get that wonderful touch
That just keeps getting better, better and
better!

WOULD YOU?

8th April '99

Would you love me as a murderer,
  If I have to become one?
Would you love me still, if I get distorted,
  And would I still be the only one?
Would you let go of me,
  If I tell you to in such a case?
However, I'm really sorry,
  For putting you in such a place.

Would you live me as a coward,
  If I step back with thought than action?
And would you care for me still,
  If I make you cry, without any intention?
Would you think badly of me
  If you find me in such a case?
However, I'm really sorry,
  For putting you in such a mess.

Will you still be ready to be by my side,
    Though after knowing I've made the mistake?
Will it then be for you for me,
    Still your love or gladness for a break?
Would you still like to rest your head on mine,
    After I become dull and stop to shine?
Would you still allow your lap for my head to rest on,
When all that was in me has gone?

Would you still love me,
    If I ask you in such a case?
However, I'm really sorry,
    For putting you in such a place.

HAVING YOU

5th Nov '99

Having you made me feel, that,
It was time I had someone special in my life
To whom I could turn to anytime . . . .
Your pool of love is so soft and safe
That brings out the ever wanting crave
To execute 'a never let go hold' on you
And keep whispering in your ears 'I love you'

With you beside me and, that,
Pure sense of trust you bring along
I just cannot help myself from going crazy
And, yes, to you forever I belong

You're the only one to whom
I can open my head without the slightest of
fears
To whom I can open my heart,
And without a shame, shed a few tears

But ultimately, it's that feeling, that,
Can pull you out of the deepest darkness
And place you among the clouds, high and free
It's the feeling, that,
Makes you want to live
This very life time and again and see . . . .

MY MEDICINE

20ᵗʰ Nov '99

When things waited for me to be done
I just wasn't with time
And when I got up and pulled myself
Those times just weren't mine
Leaving me with only myself as the judge
For my unintentional crime

What could I do?
When I fell asleep at times to be awake
What just could I do?
When I wasn't awake after the killing break

Well, one thing's for sure:
    When you cannot get a hold on yourself
    You get that chill of being laughed at
    Drawing out all the humor that's inside
    Making you sad, dead, down, and flat

It gets even harder,
When you cannot give in to some bad habits
And your love is the only one,
Who in your mind, heart and soul, as a
remedy, that fits

THE FACT

28th Nov '99

We could have been living as one
And this world could have been made intact
But we've created our own insane ways
And, yes, my love, that's the fact

Though you try hard to explain
Through your monotonous dogged act
You still find yourself trying
Since, my love, that's the fact

But isn't it sweet that it's a fact
That you and me have taken that dive
Together going deeper with time
Having each other as the reason to stay alive

Also, it's not a fact,
When you say you don't love me
It's not a fact,
If there isn't any love, in my eyes for you to see

You loved me, love me and will always love
me; for me that's the fact
I loved you, love you and will always love
you; for you that's the fact
And the fact that we have each other, all
along the way
Is the fact that's going to remain, that's
going to stay . . . .

THE DAY

24th Jan '00

There'll never be a second thought
That forever I want to be with you
And just for that special day
I'll live and even wait, if I have to

I want to see your eyes that day
See it speak out your within
I want to feel your hold that day
Feel that fearless love begin

I want to let go of myself
When you'll be breathing your love on me
And I want to make you see, that day,
That we're going to last as each other's till
eternity

So just be patient, when days seem down
Take it cool, keep your head and don't ever
frown
Because some pain we have to take along
the way
For all that is waiting in that special day;
'our day'

There'll never be a second one
And this you know far too well
And after I've got you for life
It's not a thing I have to tell

So, I want to sacrifice my sleep that day
Just to feel you sleep in peace
With no fear, jealousy or insecurity
With just in mind, that now, life's at ease

CAN I BE YOUR FRIEND

21st Mar '00

I know I've got a head
That's not good for thinking
I know I've got a heart
That's no match for feeling

So I wish I could end it all
And beside you I would fall
Into this peaceful and silent trend
I ask; can I be your friend?

I know I've got a life
That's no use of living
I know I've got goals to reach
That seems all so punishing

Nothing comes,
Even when I scratch my head
But my vision is fixed
On this path ahead

So I wish I was a piece of glare
With a mind dumb and so rare
And in this peaceful and silent trend
I still ask; can I be your friend?

SING FOR YOU

30th Mar '00

Had to run it many times
As I had to save the drive
And I wanted those lines
From my heart till you to arrive

And at last I found myself ready
Though I had to memorize a while
And this effort was no effort at all
When I got to see that sparkle and you smile

When I sang you that song
With you resting on the marble behind
Making you sit in front of me
With heart to heart and mind to mind

After all, I wanted those lines; from my heart
till you to arrive . . . .

That's not the best I can give
For that I'll have to fight for a while
And this effort will become some effort after
all
Maybe, I still can get to see that sparkle and
you smile

When I sing you that song again
With you resting by my side
Making you feel near to me
With soul to soul and ever together; never
divide

THE DAY I'LL MISS YOU SO MUCH

29th July '00

It just wasn't like the other days
When the air carried the smell of you
When I could capture you all of myself, in my eyes
Never ever thought I had a miss coming through

And when there's an absence of your touch
I feel it's a day I'm missing you so much

Every moment seems like the scene,
Through a foggy pane
Yes, I'm sad and I'm down,
But I'm not going insane . . . .

Since I have to be ready for the day I'll miss you so much
And when there'll be an absence of your touch,
It'll be the day I'll miss you so much . . . .

I might hear you call me out
Though you're nowhere near about
Emerging from the vibes when you beat
within me
And if that day was to end
My heart would burst and then
My eyes would love to fail; if you're there to
see

And when there's an absence of your touch
I feel it's a day I'm missing you so much

I DON'T KNOW HOW TO LOVE
6th Sep '00

When I walk away, leaving you behind
Without a thought, and just being blind
Hope you'll forgive me, because I don't know
how to love . . .

I should've stayed and made you smile
But you know my try, is only for a while
Because I don't know how to love . . . .

When I shout at you, without caring and
you're not dry
And when I forget, that sometimes you need
to cry
Hope you'll still love me, because I don't
know how to love . . . .

I should've talked sweet and pushed your
sadness afar
But you know my attitude is like a
complicated bar
And, yes, I don't know how to love . . . .

When I stand dumb, all to myself
Without saying anything, that could be of
your help
Hope you'll still see me, because I don't know
how to love

I should've held you close and made you feel
at peace
But all I'm able to do, is take you far from ease
Hope you'll still forgive me, because I don't
know how to love . . . .

I still feel the same for you and I love you
the way you are
It's sometimes that I mistreat you, but you're
always my glowing star . . . .

LOSING AS ALWAYS

18th Jan '01

When tears roll down
On thinking about you
I wonder if I'm growing weaker

And in these days
Missing and far from you
I can't help myself, from losing as always . . . .

When thoughts go flying
On thinking about you
I wonder if I'm going insane

But in these days
Craving; with you in my mind
I can't help myself, from losing as always . . . .

Losing as always,
    When it comes to having you
    In me, when I close my eyes
Losing as always,
    When it comes to dreaming of you
    By my side, when I close my eyes . . . .

When this heart cries
On thinking about you
I wonder if I'm going to collapse

And in these days
Feeling; deep and strong for you
I can't help myself, from losing as always . . . .

When I make my wishes
On thinking about you
I wonder if I'm asking too much

But in these days
Hoping for the gifted revival
I can't help myself, from losing as always . . . .

Losing as always,
 When it comes to having you
 With me, in our world relishing
Losing as always,
 When it comes to seeing you; Jumping,
dancing and smiling . . . .

APOLOGIES

4th June '01

If my madness, anytime,
Gets into your head
Just give it a way out; I'm still within sanity
If what I say, somewhere,
Makes you feel dead
Just take a breath; it's all vanity

Since I'll never mean to, never ever dream to
Never ever want to, ever hurt you
And if my disposition is filled with disease
Please accept, my humble apologies

If my ignorance, at times,
Kills the care in you
Just hold on a bit; you're still in my thought
If I can't take, the steps,
Which I ought to take
Just don't go away; then, it's your smile I
sought

Since I'll never mean to, never ever dream to
Never ever want to, ever hurt you
And if my disposition is filled with disease
Please accept, my humble apologies

YOU AND ME

9th June '01

I will never know
How I get the words
When it comes to talking to you
But I'll always have a doubt on my heart

And it's alright, and it's fine
As long as it makes you smile
It's alright and it's fine
Even if it's just for a while

Since that's all that's needed
For a place in forever; at the back of my mind

I will never come to know
How I get so much
Of every bits and pieces of you
But I'll always know, they belong to your heart

And it's alright, and it's fine
As long as it makes you smile
It's alright and it's fine
Even if it's just for a while

Since that is all that I need
For a place in forever; somewhere in your mind

PERSPECTIVE

26th Sep '01

Now, every kiss will weigh me down
Every tender touch will send me round
    My mind in a way it was not
Now, there will be a doubt every time
I look into your eyes, for that shine
    Not wanting to lose, what I've got

And if only there was a way
To grant understanding; to guide you through
my mind
Nothing to go astray;
Far from illusions of any kind . . . .

Why did you show the side of you?
I found too good to be true;
    For my mind to contemplate
Why did you take such risks?
(Knowing I could fail); in whisks
    Not logical in any rate

And if only there was a way
To undo apathy and guide you through your
heart
Nothing to go astray;
And very close as one, with the actual part . . . .

FEELING OF ETERNITY

30th Oct '01

May you two from now on
Start each day with a kiss
Saying to yourself
In your silent promise

That you'll never let love fade away
The love you felt the very first day
When you had met each other
And your hearts felt the singularity
Knowing that you were taken over
By the feeling of eternity

May you two be forever
Be blessed and guarded by angels
And may your love grow strong
With every toll of the bells

And do start each day with a kiss
Saying to each other, in that silent promise

That you'll never let love fade away
The love you felt the very first day
When you had met each other
And your hearts felt the singularity
Knowing that you were taken over
By the feeling of eternity

May heaven bestow itself, on earth for the
two of you . . . .
And do start each day with a kiss
Saying to each other, in that silent promise

That you'll never let love fade away
The love you felt the very first day
    When you had met each other
    And your hearts felt the singularity
    Knowing that you were taken over
    By the feeling of eternity

YOU'RE NOT GETTING ANYWHERE

28th Nov '01

So you want to know
What the bottom line is
Of life, and the fiasco
Of the bliss

Then you better start
On getting away
As I haven't got
Anything to say
Any more that to say,
You're not getting anywhere . . . .

So you want to see
What the actual picture looks like
What before approaching
Your final strike

Then you better brace
For the blow
As I cannot face
With nothing to show
Apart from when I say,
You're not getting anywhere . . . .

So you want to search
The meaning to all of this
Of life, and the fiasco
Of the bliss

Then you better expect
It so appear blunt
As I never could
Remove the shunt
Then hope you're not sorry
Since that's a fact
As I tell you
About the healing act
When I say, you're not getting anywhere . . . .

SMILE

27th Dec '01

I see your face
In front of the doorway to my thoughts
How then could I think, of anything else?

Even if I tried
I know I'd fail
Because, then you would smile
Yes! Because, then you would smile

Days have never been so unwanted
Is comes with isolation now
And nights in ache I pass
But I don't know how

Maybe it's for your smile
Maybe it's for your smile

Because, even if I tried
Just to fail
I know you would smile
Yes! I know you would smile

I see your face
In front of the doorway to my thoughts
How then could I think, of anything else?

WELL!

29th May '02

I heard you died long before
Up in your cell, lone and sure
I thought that you would wait for me
The disillusion, I couldn't see

Well! Time, don't take me low
Well! Time, don't take me low

I don't get, why you have to say
You don't have, what it takes to stay
See those weed grow fat each day
Then maybe, you would like to say

Well! Time, don't take me low
Well! Time, don't take me low
In you I'm going to flow
In you I'm going to flow

So then you left your jelly bare
Off with bone to field the scare
And wide mouth idiots I cannot bear
Wish their tongues, I could prepare

Well! Maybe, I should stay at home
Well! Maybe, I should stay at home

If life's a joke, then laugh along
Take a break and cry a song
And think of all your love and fun
So don't you ever take the gun

Well! Your fingers should've froze
Well! Your fingers should've froze

And time, don't take me low
Well! Time, don't take me low
In you I'm going to flow
In you I'm going to flow

HEAVEN LOADED

15th Nov '03

Well it freaks me out
To think about
The times we let go to waste
Standing on delusions
Softer than paste, formless as paste

The days when I lived
On the norms
I thought and executed
Never realizing, I'd be losing
Someone, heaven loaded
Someone, heaven loaded

And it just freaks me out
To think about
Where we'd have been bound
If all of this
Hadn't come around

So, on the palette of my heart and soul
I place the colors of everything in me
For those who will be born
Eventually
And with that, I surrender the entire me
For someone, heaven loaded
To someone, heaven loaded

BLINKED AND DENIED

14th Mar '03

As the days go by
I begin to see
The faded part of life
Remaining inside of me

Well, then I close my eyes
And try to steal a sleep
Then there's a nail through my heart
And it starts the weep

And you sure could
Tell me why
You don't enter my dreams
And save me a cry

And into the days
When darkness arrived
It was you who
Blinked and denied

Every time I run
In your direction to preach
You seem to be just a step
Away from my reach

And you sure could
Tell me why
You don't enter my dreams
And save me a cry

And into the days
When darkness arrived
It was you who
Blinked and denied

NEVER LET YOU GO AWAY

21st Nov '03

I've seen you fly across the ocean
With the cape of your naturality
Every time you've climbed a hill
I've seen you do it with utmost sensibility

And I'd have never let you go away
Would've placed a hill or two, in front of you,
Just to see you climb then away
But never would've let you go away

I've seen you fight hearts down
Against the river from the gateways to your
soul
And throughout the odd times you've had
I've seen the loss taking its toll

And I'd have never let you go away
Would've placed a hurt or two, inside of you,
Just to see you fight them away
But never would've let you go away

WAITING FOR THE RENDEZVOUS

7th Oct '04

You live in my mind
On a canvas drawn by my imagination
Where the colors
Are created by my anticipation
To you being in real

And as assistance
It's just your voice that there is

And I'm wondering
How and where this will go to?
And I'm waiting
Waiting for the rendezvous

And it's in my head
I'm living among my presentiments
Fueled by rehearsals
And wishful experiments
To my being unreal

And as assistance
It's just your voice that there is

And I'm wondering
Would it be too good to be true?
As I'm waiting
Waiting for the rendezvous

NOT ME

12th May '06

I could tell you
I could be with you
Till eternity
If it be

Teach you lessons
Of my seasons
Of how it's bright
Then out of sight

From momentary excellence
To my mental pestilence
I hope you see,
Before I sweep you off your feet . . . .

I could indeed say
That I would stay
Whenever you fall
But I would stall

Teach you curses
In verses, verses
To add to your anger
Like your new found stranger

From my disguised assistance
To your mental turbulence
I hope you see,
Before I sweep you off your feet . . . .

IT WOULD BE YOU

12th Oct '08

If the sunlight asks
As I wake up in the morning
Whom do you want to see?
   It would be you

If the steps I take asks
As I start off my day
Whom do you want to be beside?
   It would be you

If the air begins to ask
As I take it in for survival
Whom do you want to be my substitute?
   It would be you

If the songs that I listen to asks
As I try to find in their melody
Whom do you want to sing and write for?
   It would be you

If the moon starts to ask
As I see it stand in the pool of the sky
Whom would you be with, in the pool of love?
   It would be you
   It would be you
   It would be you

DRIFTING ACROSS

11th Oct '13

Drifting across, the shadows in my mind
I got a feeling, must be the thoughts of you
Holding me together,
    In the toughest times around . . . .

Shifting along, there's something I try to find
I got a feeling, must be to do with you
Keeping me forever,
    In the moments so sound . . . .

And this could be the reason,
    for my being,
    what I'm seeing
    and I'm feeling,
    and what I'm believing . . . .

Thinking about, everything that's about to fall
I got a feeling, my savior would be you
For me you'd be everywhere,
    No less an Angel sent from above . . . .

Moving ahead, with the chance of losing it all
I got a feeling, my only hope would be you
To bring me back from nowhere,
    Into the warm embrace of your love . . . .

And this could be the reason,
　　for my being,
　　what I'm seeing
　　and I'm feeling,
　　and what I'm believing . . . .

DEDICATIONS

TO A DEAR LADY

8th Jan '00

I know you're trying to play it safe
By leaving no loops for hooks that could pull
But later, knowing that I was a blunt one
Hope regret's not the one keeping your mind
full

You play your trump cards often at me
So no one aims their flesh gun at you
But, dear lady, do remember
I've got my trump cards too, just like you do

But I'd like to keep them in deep slumber
As I got no grudge against you, do remember
No ill conscience either to waste my time
Planning useless plots with every chime

And it's obvious on your part
Positivity is hard for you to start
But what may be, you are to me still dear
I wish in your mind, no place for fear . . . .

MY LADY ON AIR

20th Oct '01

Well I wonder
How you look
Oh! Lady with that sweet voice
Well my thoughts
You sure have took
Oh! Lady with that sweet voice

And I don't know if we'll ever get
Some moment to share
But you'll always be my,
My lady on air . . . .

And I wonder
When you smile
Do you put to shame the air around you?
I wonder
When you laugh
The devil might get smothered too . . . .

And I don't know if we'll ever get
Some moment to share
But you'll always be my,
My lady on air . . . .

You're the one
Who steals the show
Oh! Lady with that sweet voice
You're the only one
Who doesn't know
Oh! Lady with that sweet voice

And I don't know if we'll ever get
Some moment to share
But you'll always be my,
My lady on air . . . .
My lady on air . . . .

MAMEH

16th Nov '01

Now that you've gone, away
Leaving our minds in disarray
What's there, left to pray
You'll never come back, anyway

Is there a way for you to come back?

Because I can't cross the sky,
And steal you from wherever in heaven you
are, wherever in heaven you are

Life never helped you to unwind
The mysteries of your mind
Not that you've gone, behind
Just how could we find

A way to bring you back, a way to bring you
back . . . .

Because I can't tear the sky,
And steal you from wherever in heaven you
are, wherever in heaven you are

OF CONVERSATIONS

12th Dec '01

I closed my eyes
For a touch of relief
But my mind was alive
And I was again in grief

Since I could see him still talking
About things I couldn't get
I didn't care; I could see a heart
Ever so perfect

If only you could cut down, on the reasons
to sulk
If only you could cut down, on the reasons
to sulk

Now I've closed my eyes
Sure of the relief
But I feel open in mind
There's again that grief

Since I can sense him still giving
Words of wisdom I wished to get
But I didn't care; I could still see
A heart ever so perfect

If only you could cut down, on the reasons
to sulk
If only you could cut down, on the reasons
to sulk

QUEEN OF HILLS

19th Jan '02

This place is as sweet as chill
Every time it's the same feel
Maybe, I burned like the sun
But I was soothed in every turn
I got a shade, and a smile
Maybe flamy feathers, fragile
I was caught by the whirlpool
Now, I don't care if I am a fool,
    Since I like the taste of the spin
    I like the taste of the spin
    I get from Darjeeling . . . .

KATHMANDUCATION

20th Mar '02

The name just might be able to
Steal your imagination
And everyone over here
Dream of some clean air inhalation
And if you are in these kinds of dreams, it's
Kathmanducation

Hey outside, blind chair holders
Clear away your view of duty
Citizens let come, will you march ahead
In the name of humanity

Performing to come, from body to soul
Let's dream of Kathmanducation; dream of
Kathmanducation

The household AC may remind you
Of the varying constitution
But *Maiti Nepal's* doing a job
That doesn't need admiration
And if there's still a little hope, it's
Kathmanducation

She has seen such carnage
That has made the *Marg* so lifeless
And 1974 AD, can you hear your song
Making even beyond this place
And another one wasn't far away, in
Kathmanducation

Hey, let us just stop these shootings
For the sake of one short duration
Even Everest wouldn't have thought
It would meet the new generation

Performing to come, from body to soul
Let's dream of Kathmanducation; dream of
Kathmanducation

Our other side is as good as
It can be in any other location
And if your ears are open
Listen at 19, K.A.T.H. modulation
And even *sankatkal* couldn't save the world,
from *Kathmanducation*

Hey outside, blind chair holders
Clear away your view of duty
Citizens let come, will you march ahead
In the name of humanity

Performing to come, from body to soul
Let's dream of Kathmanducation; dream of
Kathmanducation

Performing to come, from body to soul
Let's dream of Kathmanducation; dream of
Kathmanducation

MY FLEET OF WHISTLES

28th Mar '02

The look of innocence
And all I want, is to remain as a child
Though time, knows no reversibility
Like, somewhere from the wild
    I was turned back into one
    I was turned back into one;
    In front of my first whistle . . . .

But now,
The sense of innocence
Seems to test the patience you need to sow
And strange as it is
You wish that in a flash you could grow

And I know soon I will age
And if I keep up this craze
This aging will be sweet
Seeing myself old, in front of my fleet

In front of my fleet . . . .

HEY, MR. JOSHI

27th Apr '02

Hey Mr. Joshi
You're the Genie
Of countless mines and kin
So Mr. Joshi
As you see
You can forget about your sin

Since you have no Saturdays
And so much for the government's grace
Just bury the irony
As you're still the Genie

Hey Mr. Joshi
When will you let me?
Drive your black CBZ
And maybe,
On the day I'm free
To soar the road to be

Since I lack the necessary paper stuff
And so much for the ability to bluff
Let's bury the irony
Let me call you Genie

Hey Mr. Joshi
Sad as you can see
There're not many words for gratitude
So Mr. Joshi
As you can see
All I got is my attitude

Since I'll never be mad at you
So much for things you've done and will do
Just bury the irony
And let me call you Genie
As you are the Genie

YOUR CHILD'S STARTED TO ROCK

30ᵗʰ July '02

Come on and dance mamma
Your child's started to rock
Jump and smile papa
Your child's started to rock

Don't you worry,
If she cannot read
Be happy and
Get her what she needs
Since your child's started to rock

She will be
A big name one day
Make you proud
For the rest of the way

So, don't you worry
If she cannot read
Be happy and
Get her what she needs

All you have to do
Is listen to her grooves
Just open your eyes
And feel her moves

And above all, don't you worry
If she cannot read
Be happy and
Get her what she needs
Since your child's started to rock

PAPER FIREFLIES

14th Nov '06

With no time for dreams
Who dared to think about tomorrow
In leaded display and screams
All you got for free was sorrow

With nothing to let you
Go back and make time that's frozen
When every birth was met
With freedom robbed by the dozen

And under metal frames and lying low
You are far from the ascending glow . . . .
Of your paper fireflies
Of your paper fireflies . . . .

SHORT STORIES, ARTICLES, ONE-ACT PLAY

MY OWN TOMBSTONE

'05 ~ '06

Every morning, his acknowledgement
of waking up obediently to the alarm,
would be followed by his usual routine of
freshening up, stretching his wary muscles
and his daily prayer. Then at 6:00 am, he
would go for his run. He used to change the
route every other day, in accordance to his
friend's suggestion that in due time would
make Amrit familiar with different streets
and landmarks around. However, there
was one section of his jogging route that he
never altered. It was, 'the last stretch'; as he
liked to call it. He was totally oblivious to
how this practice would change his outlook
on life forever.

Prior to his jogging sessions, Amrit was
unaware of most places in town. Now,
he is no stranger to most of them. His
starting point would always be *Baluwatar*,
and would always end via *Maharajgunj*,
rounding up the bend that situated a
two-storied blue house: this was along 'the
last stretch.' He had named this bend as
'corner-16', as he had decided to visit this

house, on the sixteenth day from his first run. Today happened to be that day.

Being shy by nature, he had succeeded easily in bypassing what he had to do for the last fifteen days. But he also knew that this was something he had to do. He was simply responding to the voice from within and he wanted to make sure that the voice would win today. As he neared 'corner-16', anticipation of things to follow, frisson of excitement; you name it, had had the better of him. He sweated twice as hard today. It was then that he had to rely on every bit of recollection of in the past that had demanded immense courage. Eventually, he saw the boy. Amrit smiled and signaled to the boy that he wanted to come in. In return, the boy pointed towards his right signaling the entrance.

The means of initiation of communing with the interior was situated beside a corrugated iron gate: very unusual. It was answered by a beautiful lady with her lengthy hair neatly plaited. "Yes," she asked.

"Um . . . good morning. My name is Amrit, Amrit Shrestha. I always happen to see this sweet little boy by that window of yours, and, uh . . . . and, I was wondering if I could meet him. It has been fifteen days, already, since we've just exchanged smiles . . . . hah . . . so . . . ." he said pointing to the window, getting fidgety.

"Oh! So it's you then! My son had mentioned about someone who always smiled at him while passing by . . . . So, it's you. Come on in." She guided Amrit to the house through a well attended garden. Amongst the psychedelic array of flowers, rows of bushes trimmed to precision, bricks embedded into the ground in a saw tooth format playing the hedging role, the thing that stood out was the fountain. It stood below a huge rubber plant at the far corner—statue of Cupid, smiling, and with the water running down straight from the tip of his arrow, how Amrit wished it multiplied and planted itself in places of scarcity. Strangely, he felt the statue's countenance correlate with his wish. "It's beautiful . . . . awesome," Amrit exclaimed.

"Thank you," she said. "The garden work helps to calm myself down. Well my son doesn't get visited that often. As for you, I hope you won't regret your decision to meet him." As she said this, she opened the main door to the house. Though, it was apparent by now, that the boy was her son, Amrit on the other hand, couldn't quite make anything of what she had just said or meant.

"Please make yourself comfortable while I'll go get Amar," she said as they entered. Hopping her way up the short flight of steps that probably let to the other room, she stopped all of sudden, turned around to face Amrit and said, "My son." She smiled and went on.

"So, Amar is his name," Amrit said to himself looking around the room still unable to figure out what she had meant earlier, and why she had to go and get him. Couldn't she have just called out his name? Amar? Amu? *Chora*?

The room was spacious and decorated with marvelous artifacts. Apart from how satisfying they were to view, Amrit had no idea, whatsoever, what they were nor knew any related anecdotes. Then a clanky sound brought his mind back to the rendezvous, which had progressed with a rather mysterious feel; not much to his liking. Then there he was, in front of him, arriving . . . . in fact, rolling by. Yes, rolling by, assisted by his mother, especially on the steps. Amrit's mind went back to the sight of the boy seated on a silver chair by the window. The silver chair turned out to be Amar's wheelchair.

Amrit sprang up: it was like he had never wanted to be seated in the first place. His body stiffened and his eyes were fixed on Amar like needles to a magnet. Somehow, they wanted to see something else. The only thing he hoped of now, was that nobody spoke a word, and like many hopes already shattered, today Amrit's was one.

"Amar, this is Amrit and Amrit this is my son Amar," she introduced them to each other. "Why don't you two take it further than the smile, while I'll go and fix us something to eat, alright?" she rolled Amar a couple of inches closer to Amrit and headed for the kitchen, fearing a repeat of what had happened so many times long, long ago.

Slowly, Amrit started to breathe deep trying to conceal the merest of hint trying to. But, he couldn't cope with the situation. Finally, Amar said, "So we both have the same initials right?" breaking the silence and being far from rhetorical.

". . . . Yes . . . . ," Amrit said and smiled, but the smile wasn't the same. He didn't know what to say after that.

"Please sit down will you, you're scaring me. You're looking like a mummy . . . . without the wrappings, of course," said Amar rather humorously.

Amrit did sit down. He knew he had to snap out of this trance as soon as he could. "So . . . . how old are you?" he asked.

"Sixteen," replied Amar.

"Sixteen . . . right," repeated Amrit, and once again felt the quivering return.

Just then Amar's mother walked in with a tray full of biscuits, sandwiches and tea. Strangely, her arrival subdued Amrit's restlessness. Maybe it was the tray and its contents. Indeed it was, because chewing had Amrit completely at ease; at last. Unfortunately, it wasn't to last long.

"Well, I'll take it that you've been wondering about Amar being in a wheelchair," Amar's mother started. "He has been like this from birth. His legs don't move from knee below. In fact it has moved up to his knees." She said with great difficulty and reluctance to use the word paralysis.

Unfortunately, that was it. Amrit couldn't take it any longer. His entire body started to ache, as if a spasm takeover was taking place. He stood up like a piece of bread out of a toaster with loose springs and said, "Um . . . . sorry . . . . but . . . , I have to leave," and without waiting for any response he sped out of the house onto the main road. The very road he thought for a while he should've stuck to.

He then set off at a brisk pace. Gradually, everything started to make sense, from the silver chair in which Amar happened to be seated every morning, to each and every statement his mother had made, and with each flash of realization his pace quickened, until he found himself racing to his room. His inability to establish any contention to the evolving argument on 'Why?' led to the remembrance of his friend Suroj: an atheist. He then grew conscious of the agnosticism barging in.

On arriving home, his mother enquired on his dreadful state. He desired to express his downheartedness, surrender to the protection of her embrace and cry. But his inability to do so resulted to a peculiar sensation of his heart changing into a dank site, constantly swelling, on each victory he gained over his emotional outburst.
Amrit evaded further questions by constructing a false headache and a need to sleep as a remedy. Far from it; later that night, lying on his bed, Amrit had pondered over what Amar's mother had meant when she had said 'it has moved up to his knees.'

Meanwhile at the blue house, what Amar's mother had feared came true.

"There goes another on *hai* mummy . . . . but after a long, long time!" Amar said after Amrit had left.

"Yes son, but the good thing was, he wasn't any of our family members," she said strengthening herself, observing how Amar nullified each arising disappointment by a smile to its name.

*

Next day, as always, Amar sat by the window but Amrit didn't pass by. Far out in the sky he could see scattered white babies being put to sleep under a widespread black blanket. It was going to rain. At that very moment, the doorbell rang. After sometime, Amar's mother walked in accompanied by Amrit. They both smiled on seeing each other. This time it was the same old smile.

"I'm sorry I ran out like that yesterday," Amrit apologized.

"It's alright. It's not the first time that has happened to me," said Amar and smiled again. The downpour began. It fell upon the blue house like a persistent applause.

"Do you like the rain, Amar?" asked Amrit.

"Yes . . . . I think I do," replied Amar.

"Great . . . . and aunty, do you like the rain?"

"Yes . . . . I think I do too, now," she said overwhelmed by her son's happiness.

The dark sky didn't matter now; only the rain did. This was to be the beginning of their deep friendship.

In days to come, under Amrit's escort, Amar enjoyed what his town had to offer. It was like unwrapping gifts, every day; gifts he didn't know about. They would eat Amar's favorite dishes as well as try Amrit's choices, in all known and unknown centers they could. They even went to see movies. Amar liked animation and special effects. Yesterday, they had seen 'Alien vs. Predator' at Jai Nepal hall and not to mentions, he was over the moon. Amrit relished every moment of it. But ironically, it was like every good thing came with a price.

As days went by, Amrit also came to know some dreadful facts concerning Amar's paralysis: it was of those spreading paralysis, and had to be treated as soon as possible. The problem was that proper treatment could only be done abroad and was very expensive. The medication he was on only slowed the spread to some extent. Despite all these horrifying facts, Amrit was focused on having as much good time with Amar as was feasible.

*

That night hosted a clear sky; it appeared to have obliged to the readiness of the stars to shed their inhibitions. Both of them were witnessing this grand white-glittered-black from the terrace of Amrit's house. Then Amrit asked, "Hey Amar, what is the one thing you want?"

"My own tombstone," answered Amar almost instantaneously.

Astonished Amrit turned towards Amar and asked, "Why do you say so?"

"So that people can visit me even after I die. That way I won't be lonely."

"Oh! Come on, you're just sixteen years old *yaar*."

"Yah! Tell that to the man my mum was talking to this morning. I heard it all, you know. Never saw mum so worried."

Amrit sensed the pain in his voice, and felt his own gripping. Determined not to let the miasma of depression spread, he said, "But then you'll need to have a foreign citizenship or be abroad for that, isn't it? Anyway, let's say you have one . . . . Where would you like to have your tombstone then?"

"In U.S.A. I saw this big cemetery with lots of tombstones, on T.V., sometime back. I would like to have my own there, so even if I don't have a visitor, I could see other tombstones being visited." Saying this Amar smiled. He had thought about the whole caboodle.

Amrit was speechless. This had predisposed him to thinking of ways to fulfill Amar's wish.

For the next couple of weeks, Amrit got busy with his friends on the internet. With the hard earned consent of Amar's mother, they were searching for someone willing to adopt Amar, even after hearing out his case. It wasn't easy, but their hard work paid off in the form of Mr. and Mrs. Tyler. They had a son and two daughters. Amrit had made sure that Amar had a healthy number of visitors, though it was troublesome even thinking about it

*

It had already been a week since Mr. Tyler and one of his daughters had been in town.

They had come to meet Amar, and for the necessary legalities taken care of by an NGO office at *Putalisadak*. It was one of those offices Amrit had come to know about during his run. He doesn't find the need to run nowadays.

One day, when Amrit took Amar out for a stroll, he was touched by what Amar said. He said, "I'm going to change my name from Amar to Arma, Arma Tyler." When asked why, he said, "I don't want you to think, life is ironic. Beside, Arma sounds more foreign right?" he smiled, and that was to be their last time together.

*

A couple of months after Amar's departure, Amrit came to know that the operation hadn't come off. For the first time his friends saw him cry. They let him.

Now Amar lies in the very cemetery he had talked about, in U.S.A., and among many other tombstones, he has his own, engraved:

ARMA TYLER
b. 20th August 1990 d. 18th March 2007
RELATED TO ANYONE WHO VISITS
R.I.P.

LAND OF WISHES

25th Sep '06

It was the age of mysticism and transcendental journeys, and for a sage of his reputation and knowledge, the recurring feeling of dissatisfaction was extremely uncharacteristic and annoying. *Vrindhakeshari*, where he had lived for the last eighty nine years suddenly seemed inadequate, and he could not recall a single day when he had felt as such. He had grown up under the wise guidance of his father *Bhramikdeva* and floating to all imaginable spaces in the enchanting stories told by his mother *Sukinahdevi*. They had named him *Bhumirath*, having crawled outside and walked back with two fistfuls of dry earth right after his birth. The incident was like a question to his parents on why the land around was so barren. As a matter of fact, the barrenness around his small hut where he and disciples lived was one of the several reasons behind his dissatisfaction of not how things had been, but were.

The numerable status of trees and sparse vegetation added to his silent lament. His wisdom prevented him from any form of disclosure. But it was at night that brought him the greatest of despairs, when he along with his disciples *Kritagyata, Sushantikala,* and *Caitanya* had to compromise for space inside his small hut divided in two by a saffron drape.

Sushantikala was the youngest of the three and had tresses that exemplified her elegance and liveliness. She would be the first to get up every morning, and when she undid the saffron drape *Bhumirath* would bless her every time. *Bhumirath* soon realized that the smallness of his hut was the principal reason behind his dissatisfaction. He could have changed everything with his power for the better, but his profound insights indicated it was not that simple. The intrusion by this peculiar ailment was of a large scale with deep roots and required an equally drastic antidote to nullify it. So, one morning, as soon as *Sushantikala* undid the drape, much to the astonishment of his disciples, *Bhumirath* revealed his decision to leave for *Manishankar* hill to undergo *'tapasya'*. To the ensuing queries of his disciples, especially *Kritagyata, Bhumirath,* but maintained a charming smile.

Ultimately, after a moment of silence *Caitanya* said, "If *swami* desires *tapasya*, then there certainly must be a consequential reason behind his decision. We all must respect it and be patient."

Bhumirath was pleased to witness the development of his disciple and said, "I see you are growing wiser by the day, *Caitanya*." *Kritagyata* and *Sushantikala* followed with smiles and their countenance clearly expressed that now, they were void of any doubts. And for a moment *Bhumirath* wanted to exchange states with his disciples. The three knelt in reverence and *Bhumirath* blessed them.

The night before his decided departure, *Bhumirath* was restless and could not sleep. He opened his eyes for a solution and then closed them to think about his father and mother. His father's voice reverberated inside his mind on the advice, '*Bhumirath, my son, be careful in what you ask; a majestic opportunity lies ahead for you to understand . . . Bhumirath, my son, be careful in what you ask; a majestic opportunity lies a . . .*' Gradually, much to the relief of *Bhumirath,* his mother's voice started to gain decibel. When her talking became audible, he realized that she was narrating his favorite story about how a girl named *Trishnahuti* learned to make the most of whatever she had. *Bhumirath* smiled and soon floated away into a much needed state of slumber.

*

Bhumirath's journey to *Manishankar* hill was far from pleasant. Half way through his journey he realized that he had been putting up a tireless effort to contemplate any logical explanations behind the benevolence of the God of Creation, *Brahma,* over his neighborhood. Unable to conjure up any explanation he advanced the rest of the journey with his eyes closed, summoning up his *divya shakti.*

On reaching *Manishankar* hill *Bhumirath* chose the only *peepal* tree around with a single surviving leaf and spoke to it, "Not long my friend . . . not long. You shall be green and full of life, again, soon." He took up the *padmasana,* chanted *Om* five times, half-closed his eyes, and initiated his *tapasya* with the subsequent incantations formulated in honor of Lord *Brahma.*

In the days, months, and years to follow, *Vrindhakeshari* had to withstand a conglomeration of unusual activities. There were fiery hurricanes, demonic stampedes, and icicle eruptions. *Bhumirath* knew that the one to orchestrate such mayhem was none other than *Pralayasur,* the demon whom *Bhumirath* had confined to the deepest of darkness feared by every demons, some forty years ago. It was a victory that had not only saved the world from a complete demonic dominance, but also had won *Bhumirath* the recognition by Lord *Shiva*. From that day onwards he was also to be known as *Jatadhara,* for he was granted the power to produce water from the top of his layered hair; an ability similar to Lord *Shiva's*. *Bhumirath* persisted with his tapasya and so did *Pralayasur* with his chaos. Whatever vegetation and wildlife there were, were either frozen or instantly transformed into ashes. *Bhumirath,* however, was undeterred. He knew their rejuvenation was inevitable.

Back at the small hut, it was up to *Kritagyata* to create an orb of protection around the hut and for *Sushantikala* and *Caitanya* to sustain its existence until required. The orb was powerful enough to protect them and the small hut from the varied onslaught of *Pralayasur*. *Bhumirath* and taught them well. They proved themselves worthy disciples of *Jatadhara Bhumirath.*

*

In the prolonged demonic destruction not a single living entity survived. All that was left of *Vrindhakeshari* was *Bhumirath* and the peepal tree with the single surviving leaf, his small hut, and his three disciples inside the orb of protection. *Pralayasur's* tantrum didn't cease. His demons had initiated the ultimate distraction, *danava nritya*; the 'demon dance', on the ashes that blanketed the vicinity of *Bhumirath*. Their dancing had made the ambience dark as their intentions. The ashes floated like evil spirits, responding faithfully to the movements of the demons and the beats of their dance. Their swiveling ascent and virulent spread was bound to engulf the entire atmosphere into a frenzy of depletion. But evil was never to be victorious.

A strand of light pierced the darkness, contracted into a tiny sparkle, and then exploded into a silent burst of brightness of such intensity that all the ashes transformed into a psychedelic shower of flowers. The frozen life forms were thawed back into existence and the dancing demons morphed into a random array of hedges. Then, there was the anguished cry of *Pralayasur* that epitomized a missed opportunity. He knew he could never destroy *Bhumirath* in his full consciousness. He realized that he had missed the opportunity to resurface. However, on the other hand, *Bhumirath* was not to miss his opportunity of a lifetime. He kept his concentration intact.

When all the chaos had subsided with brightness all around, a floating lotus appeared in front of *Bhumirath*. On the lotus was seated Lord *Brahma*. He said in his resonating voice, *"Bhumirath,* dear *Bhumirath,* open your eyes. Open your eyes and ask what you desire my son."

Bhumirath was so overwhelmed by the presence of Lord *Brahma* that for a moment he forgot what he actually wanted. Regaining composure he answered, *"Pranaam Bhagawan, pranaam . . .* I ask of you that may my land be a land of wishes."

"Is that what you really want *Bhumirath?"*

"Yes *Bhagawan.* I'd like my land to be a land of wishes."

Lord *Brahma* smiled wisely and said, "Very well then my son. *Tathastu!"*

After Lord *Brahma* had returned to the heavenly dimensions *Bhumirath* stood up slowly, satisfied by the thought that he had made the most of the opportunity he had been granted. He was ninety three years old now and could visualize *Vrindhakeshari* coming back to life like a new born. But first he had a task at hand. He faced the peepal tree he was seated with for the last four years, smiled and closed his eyes to make his first wish. Before he could complete his wish, a rustling sound made him open his eyes. Much to his amazement, he saw that the peepal tree was already full of leaves and swaying in merriment. He thought it must have been the intensity in his desire that the peepal tree came alive in advance. It never occurred to him that it was in fact the peepal tree's own wish behind the accelerated recovery. After all *Bhumirath* had asked for a land of wishes and not for a land of 'his' wishes. He was preoccupied with the smallness of his hut to ponder further over his unexpected amazement.

On his way back *Bhumirath* wished for a river and he got one. He, however, missed the formation of a ridge in the middle of his river and the eventual development of a torrent, graced by a frolicking batch of salmons. He wished for a butterfly and witnessed it fly away. He, however, missed the magical growth of a marigold and how softly his butterfly had settled down on it, only to be accompanied by another butterfly of its kind.

Finally, he was within sight of his disciples and his small hut. His disciples were pleased that their master had been successful with his *tapasya* and he in turn was pleased to realize that his disciples had successfully protected the dwelling place. No longer had *Bhumirath* stepped inside his compound that his small hut expanded into fourfold its present dimension. That night all four of them had their sweetest of dreams.

*

Early next morning it was *Sushantikala's* scream that brought *Bhumirath, Kritagyata,* and *Caitanya* back to reality. The reason behind her screaming was a warthog, persistently digging up a burrow in their compound. Before it could complete its excavation there was a thunderous roar, and out of the green hideout a lion pounced on the warthog with a single mighty leap. With the warthog safely rested between its jaws, the lion turned towards *Bhumirath.* The lion had a look of gratitude on his face.

There were just two lingering emotions after the lion disappeared into the woods; disturbed was *Bhumirath,* while awestruck were his disciples. The lion-warthog spectacle had announced the advent of several natural events they had never seen before, and all of them involved only animals of the wild.

The wise *Bhumirath* soon realized what had happened. He had realized that desires were the main cause and he thought he had done the right thing to tackle it. However, he also realized how he had missed one word in his reply to Lord *Brahma*. It was a vital word but with how things had turned up he had no regrets. In fact, on the contrary, he was rather pleased that his blunder had opened up a whole new dimension of opportunities for every living being. All they had to do was realize, and the way the animals of the wild communicated with themselves was an enigma in itself. He thought maybe the absence of realization was the reason why he had not yet witnessed a single human ignorance. No wonder what catastrophes would befall humanity had the humans, both good and evil, realized the opportunity unlocked by him. He would rather prefer that *Pralayasur* resurface since animals, lived by their necessities and never seem to go overboard; humans were a totally different prospect.

*

It had been several days since his encounter with *Brahma Dev. Bhumirath* had been trying repeatedly, without success, to remove the barrenness of a patch of land on the right side of hit *large* hut. It was by no means a necessity on his part, but still he had continued with his efforts since that was the only odd part around. His disciples also knew about his vain efforts as he used to tell them, "It seems this patch of land will never come alive." He surrendered to wisdom and immediately decided to halt his unnecessary efforts.

One day *Bhumirath* was observing the eagerness to bloom of a bud of his flower, when all of a sudden his head felt cold and wet. From the top of his head a steady trickle of water appeared ending into a soft continuum of tiny droplets that showered the flower. By now, *Bhumirath* knew what was happening. He smiled and stood still. "So . . . you too have become a part of the wishing team. You certainly are making the most of it." He said and smiled.

Suddenly, out of the corner of his eyes he saw *Kritagyata* running up to him like a messenger with a message that could not afford any delay. On reaching *Bhumirath*, *Kritagyata* said, "*Swami*, the . . . patch of . . . land . . . it has come . . . alive. Quick Swami, you must see this."

Bhumirath was a little confused and said in good humor, "Come alive? Is it dancing then, my dear *Kritagyata*? Or has it grown a pair of hands and is clapping?"

Kritagyata smiled and corrected himself, "No *Swami*. I mean there's vegetation."

Now, *Bhumirath* was surprised. He stood still though, until his flower had had her fill. After the steady trickle receded, both of them headed for the aforementioned patch of land with restless anticipation. *Bhumirath* saw *Sushantikala* and *Caitanya* standing like protectors of something very rare. Once they reached the site, what *Kritagyata* had delivered was indeed true. The patch of land had lost its barrenness to a fresh spread of grass. They all were spellbound. They marveled at the magical greenery until an unexpected rustle in the nearby hedges broke their concentration. To their relief and ecstasy, it was a deer. He slowly approached them, and once within reach started to nibble away at the fresh grass that they had found to be so fascinating. When the deer had finished eating he trotted away and all that was left of the patch of land was green spots on an ashen background. He suddenly stopped at the hedges and turned to face *Bhumirath* causing a steady trickle of water to moisten the place where he had just dined. Once again the trickle resided and the deer trotted away. *Bhumirath* in his amazement said to himself, "*Heh, Brahma dev,* it seems everything is making the most out of it!"

"Did you say something, Swami?" asked *Sushantikala.*

Bhumirath replied, "Nothing my child, nothing. Just remembering my father and telling him that I understand." Deep inside, he also knew that this could be something beyond his comprehension. Until he felt the need to seek answers again, or until he witnessed the misuse of the gift he had brought upon his land, he was happy and did not wish for anything else.

*

TWO SIDES TO A COIN?

28th Nov '04

Cubicle-9 belonged to me and my friend, Vinay. We really loved our cubicle. It was like 'our room' away from home and as I recollect, the connection between 'yin' and 'yang' and the anecdote on the feedback of our cubicle, never fail to amuse me. This is a reflection on the feedback provided on our cubicle long time ago by our friends, Jolly and Sadly.

That day was a Saturday, and we both had worked very hard in arranging our cubicle in the best way possible. Since we were looking for a positive feedback we had invited Jolly first. She was the ideal choice as she was having the time of her life with her successes in the half-yearly and mock tests, and we hadn't had to regret our choice. Though we hadn't done anything to the door, even its fading whiteness had been enough for her to see purity in it. Our bunk beds had reminded her of teamwork, co-operation and effective space management.

Though using an electric heater wasn't allowed, we used to cook noodles and sometimes a late night dinner secretively. The wirework was concealed having been forced into the crevices of adjacent ply woods that made up the ceiling. Jolly, on knowing this, had mentioned that it was a work of creativity and depicted basic survival instincts.

She had praised our bookshelves and how the books were properly arranged. She had mentioned that it was good that we respected what we read. She had enjoyed the aroma of the fresh rose on Vinay's desk, while she was almost taken over by emotion on seeing my family photo on my desk. She had admired the 'mobility arrangement' proposed by Vinay, stating that anyone could move about with ease inside the cubicle. The arrangement had the desk parallel to each other creating three vacant columns. Lastly, the mirror beside the door had a smiley face on it which had made Jolly not only smile, but laugh her heart out. She had thanked us for the invitation and I still remember how we never wanted to leave our cubicle.

Unfortunately, later that day, Sadly had arrived with our return tickets from cloud nine. She had started by saying how badly the door needed a painting and how it reminded her of her own state. She wasn't having it easy back then, balancing between two jobs and babysitting. She would say, "Well, I used to read Dennis the Menace and laugh but now I see one every day, and he makes me want to cry."

Our bunk beds had been pathetic for her. All she had said was 'how discriminating', and how one had to put that extra effort to climb to sleep, while the other could just fall down and doze away. I remember, sadly, Sadly had even enacted the 'fall down and doze' part.

On knowing about the electric heater, she had stated that we were doing something illegal and how our tuition fees did not cover for the heater usage, and that there was enough food provide by the institution. The ordered bookshelves had given her the impression that we weren't studying at all. As for the 'mobility arrangement' she had said, "What's with these huge gaps? Tell you what . . . . a Sumo wrestler could run wild in your room."

How we had wished she would just leave. She had even suggested that instead of my family photo, I should've put Einstein's picture for motivation.

Lastly, the smiley too hadn't gone well with her; for obvious reasons, sadly. After she had left, we had consoled each other by the fact that at least, she had left Vinay's rose alone.

ON PAR

29th Aug '12

Recently the word Par stuck in my mind. Of course I don't play Golf; in fact, I don't know the rules to start with. So, in the same strange and uncanny way the mind always works in, it drove me to dig a bit further into the word. To my delight it had an idiom, *'On par with something/someone'*, meaning to be equal to something/someone.

I think that is what most of us strive towards, either equaling something set like a target, or becoming like someone whom we look up to in terms of their disposition and attributes. It's also true that most of us either leave the journey of attainment in between for various reasons, or once attained hit a stalemate. Well, I'm neither a preacher nor an adviser. I'm here like anyone of you, no more different, no more familiar. Of course, stating some facts as well as sharing some thoughts like anyone of you, nothing much, nothing less.

So, on the same note, returning back to the word Par, floating along the crazy thought train of my mind, I gave up all the pros and cons that came along and interestingly hit upon an acronym of PAR which I thought I'd share with you all. Hoping, that it might amuse, help, entertain, pass your time, fill in the blanks; here it goes:

PAR—Perspective Attitude Results

How did I stumble across it? I don't have the exact idea. I told you—Crazy Train of Thoughts! And in the end it did make sense. Depending upon the Perspective you have of Life, thus would lay the corresponding foundation towards the development of your Attitude, which in turn would be the driving force behind the Results attained and experienced.

So, if you have a right and healthy Perspective of life, it would lead towards you developing a positive Attitude, which in turn would drive positive Results. Saying this—remember, nothing much, nothing less—I'll leave you all to your respective Trains of Thoughts! Crazy or Not. And yes, forget about being On Par with something or someone; just don't forget to be On Par with none other than yourself!

AFTER THE THUNDER AND THE BLACK-OUT

'06 ~ '07

STAGE DIVISION:

Divided into two sections—the center stage and the side stage (L or R).
L refers to the left portion and R refers to the right portion.

Characters:

Scene—1:

Richard—Husband of Flo. Sort of a simpleton who wants to make honest efforts, but often thinks of only by himself.

Flo—Wife of Richard. A strong headed woman with a kind heart, who wants her husband to think matters of their relationship on a mutual ground.

Scene—2:

Yoshi—Husband of **Mariko**; father of **Yuri**. A businessman who has just lost his business and is on the verge of a mental breakdown.

Mariko—Wife of **Yoshi**; mother of **Yuri**. A very calm woman with an apt foresight.

Yuri—Daughter of Yoshi and Mariko. A wise girl who likes travelling.

Scene—3:

Doctor—A doctor who has been treating **Sagar**.

Sagar—Son of **Ms. Thapa**, a kid with a big heart and who has been suffering from a serious arm infection.

Ms. Thapa—Mother of Sagar. An emotional and strong woman, who loves her son so much that at times, it gets her to believe that she can do anything for him.

SCENE—1:

Center Stage—Richard and Flo (somewhere in England)

Silence

Appear Richard and Flo

RICHARD: So, what next . . . . then? I mean, what should I do now?

FLO: Geez, Richard . . . . See, that's your problem. It's always about you, you having to do this, that.

RICHARD: What's that now? What do you mean?

FLO (raised tone): Can't you for once let go of the notion that everything has got to do with you!

RICHARD: But, but . . . you did mention that all this chaos was due to me, didn't you? So, I just want to know how could, I . . . .

FLO (strident tone): THAT'S NOT WHAT I MEANT! GOD! *(Calms down)* When will you be able to understand what I say?

RICHARD: Then my dear Flo, this calls for a celebration! *(Sarcastically)*

FLO: What the hell do you mean by that?

RICHARD: That it's a miracle we've been married for the last sixteen years without understanding!

FLO: Without you understanding me! It's my understanding of you that has kept this marriage alive, alright.

RICHARD: If that's so, then you should be able to tell me, what I should do, now . . . . that our marriage is falling apart.

FLO: There, there you go again. Let go Richard. *(In fading decibel)*

RICHARD: Let go of what? It's quite clear that I'm the problem and all I'm asking, is what can I, or should I, do to fix the problem.

FLO: Let go of blaming yourself. Marriage is something that's mutual. Something that has to have . . . . togetherness, even in thinking over stuffs. There's no . . . . I, but us. Do you understand?

RICHARD: Humph . . . . How could I, Flo? You just said I don't understand . . . understand you, or anything you say, right?

FLO: You're impossible, Richard! *(Irate)* IMPOSSIBLE! Ah . . . . Not even Heracles Pontor would be able to decipher the enigma behind the . . . the . . . . the zig-saw puzzle to making you understand what I say!

RICHARD (little irritated): Now, who the hell is this Pontor? I thought it was about me, no, us, no, me, understanding, no, not understanding . . . . Ah! Listen lady, I'm not a rocket scientist alright, and I may not have that appreciable an IQ . . . . but I sure do can UNDERSTAND!

FLO (dropped tone): What!?!

RICHARD: Please wise one, enlighten me with what I should understand, so I can undo what I did not do and do what I have to do. *(Pause)* What's necessary for me to do to . . . .

FLO (shouts): STOP! STOP! *(Decibel drops)* Stop! That's it! I mean *(Decibel rises)* THAT'S IT!

RICHARD (frustrated): What THAT'S IT DAMN IT!

Argument

FLO (shouts): I'M LEAVING! I'M LEAVING,
   YOU! YOU HEAR ME! I'M LEAVING . . . .
   YOU!

Flo preparing to leave
Flo on her way out
A thunder sounds; Flo stops
Then a black-out

SCENE—2:

*Center Stage—Yoshi, Mariko, and Yuri
   (somewhere in Japan)*

Side Stage (R)—Richard and Flo

*Richard and Flo sees what Yoshi, Mariko,
and Yuri are going through, but Yoshi,
Marko, and Yuri cannot see Richard and Flo.*

   YOSHI (sitting and sobbing): It's over
Mari. It's all over! There's nothing left. We're
bankrupt.
   MARIKO: Now come on honey, it can't
be that bad as it seems. I mean . . . *(fading
tone)*

   Brief blinking, lighting effect

Then a black-out

SCENE—3:

Center Stage—Yoshi, Mariko, and Yuri

YOSHI *(sitting and sobbing):* It's over Mari. It's all over! There's nothing left. We're bankrupt.

MARIKO: Now come on honey, it can't be that bad as it seems. I mean . . .

YOSHI: I said we're bankrupt, didn't you hear me right! WE ARE BANKRUPT! I, I, I can't believe this.

MARIKO: it's alright dear! It'll be fine. Everything will be fine.

YOSHI: The business I spent my last ten years in, is now gone. Just like that. How am I going to look after you all now?

MARIKO: It's alright Yoshi! It's alright. Calm down.

YOSHI: How am I to calm down? How?

Brief silence

YURI: Does this mean I can't go to New Zealand?

MARIKO *(scolding tone):* Yuri!

YOSHI: It's over! What am I going to do?

(Stands up, stiffens and looks around. Grabs his hair and squats.)

YOSHI: It's all over!
MARIKO *(hugging Yoshi):* Calm down dear. *(Pause)* Yuri, go get your father a glass of water.

Exit Yuri

MARIKO: It's alright dear. It's alright. We still have my account intact . . . . and we still have that land back in our village! So, calm down alright honey! Please!

Enter Yuri with water

YURI: Papa, here, drink some water. I don't want to go to New Zealand.

Yoshi springs up

YOSHI: IT'S ALL OVER! It's, it's . . . there's nothing left, nothing. *(Pause)* Nothing left for me to do now than to kill myself. Yes, yes . . . I'll . . . kill . . . myself.
MARIKO: Yoshi, no, no, stop, calm down, no Yoshi, no, no . . . . Yuri, help me. No, Yoshi, no
YURI *(choking tone):* Mummy! . . . Papa! Papa! Papa!

Mariko and Yuri approach Yoshi

Yoshi pushes them both aside
Takes out a knife from his briefcase

MARIKO: No, Yoshi. *(Cries)* No! Yo . . . shi . . .
YURI: Papa, no papa . . . *(Screams)*

Yoshi raises his knife to his throat
A thunder sounds
Then a black-out

SCENE—4:

Center Stage—Doctor, Sagar, and Ms. Thapa (somewhere in India)

Side Stage (R)—Yoshi, Mariko, and Yuri

Yoshi, Mariko, and Yuri sees what Sagar and his mum are going through, but the vice versa doesn't take place

DOCTOR: Oh! God! How am I to put this!
MS. THAPA: What does the test results say doctor?
DOCTOR: I feel extremely sad to say this, Ms. Thapa, that . . . Sagar has to have both his arms . . . amputated. *(Fading tone)*

Brief blinking lighting effect
Then a black-out

SCENE—5:

Center stage—Doctor, Sagar, and Ms. Thapa

DOCTOR: Oh! God! How am I to put this!

MS. THAPA: What does the test results say doctor?

DOCTOR: I feel extremely sad to say this, Ms. Thapa, that . . . Sagar has to have both his arms . . . amputated.

MS. THAPA: What! What do you mean by that? It's ridiculous! That can't be!

DOCTOR: I'm so sorry Ms. Thapa. I'm really . . .

MS. THAPA: NO! No, no . . . There must be another way out of this. *(Shivering)* I mean this is the twenty first century for heaven's sake, and you're the one who's supposed to . . .

DOCTOR: Ms. Thapa the amputation has to be done. Otherwise, the infection in his arms could take your son's life, maybe, within a year or two.

Brief silence
Ms. Thapa starts to cry.

DOCTOR: I'm really sorry Ms. Thapa. I really am. But it has to be done . . . for your son.

Doctor turns towards Sagar

DOCTOR: You alright Sagar?
SAGAR: It seems I must be, now, for my mum . . . you know.

Doctor places his hands on Sagar's head and turns towards Ms. Thapa

DOCTOR: Your son's a brave boy, Ms. Thapa.

Exit Doctor
The crying intensifies

SAGAR: Mumma!
MS. THAPA: I'm . . . alright.

Unable to control her emotions she continues to cry

SAGAR *(shouts):* Mumma!

Crying stops

SAGAR: Mumma! I'm the one who's going to have an amputation alright! I'm not crying. See? So, please mumma, stop crying.
MS. THAPA *(sounding strong):* Shut up! The moment I walk out of this cabin, you'll start crying like a baby. It doesn't have to be my arms. I feel your pain as much as I feel your joy. I'm your mother and I didn't carry you in my womb for nine months for nothing.

SAGAR: Yes, I know . . . you're right. I will start crying. I'm going to lose my arms, hah . . . I'll soon be armless . . . *(Starts to sob)*. What will I do . . . ? *(Cries)*

MS. THAPA *(crying tone):* Well! We can cry together . . .

She hugs her son and both of them cry
After

SAGAR: I can't even hug you back, mumma.

MS. THAPA: It's alright son! You just snuggle yourself in mine, OK!

SAGAR: I don't want to lose my arms, mumma, I don't want to lose my . . . *(Cries)*

MS.THAPA: No! I won't let you lose your arms! There must be a way out of this *(springs up)*. There has to be another option! Yes! Yes! There must be! There must be! *(Sobs)* I won't let my son lose his arms! THERE MUST BE!

SAGAR: Mumma! Mumma! MUMMA! *(Cries)*

A thunder sounds
Then a black-out

SCENE—6:

Center Stage—Sagar and Ms. Thapa

Side Stage (L)—Richard and Flo

Sagar and Ms. Thapa sees what Richard and Flo are going through, but the vice versa doesn't take place

RICHARD: So, what next . . . then? I mean, what should I do now?

FLO: Geez, Richard . . . See, that's your problem. It's always about you, you having to do this, that.

Mute
Richard and Flo continue with their enacting
Brief blinking lighting effect
Then a black-out

SCENE—7:

Center Stage—Richard and Flo

Side Stage (L)—Yoshi, Mariko, and Yuri

YOSHI: IT'S ALL OVER! It's, it's . . . there's nothing left, nothing. (Pause) Nothing left for me to do now than to kill myself. Yes, yes . . . I'll . . . kill . . . myself.

MARIKO: Yoshi, no, no, stop, calm down, no Yoshi, no, no . . . . Yuri, help me. No, Yoshi, no

YURI *(choking tone):* Mummy! Papa! Papa! Papa!

Yoshi, Mariko, and Yuri go into a freeze mode
Richard and Flo sees what they are going through

RICHARD: Geez! Poor guy! He's lost everything! And I was thinking, who could be in a worse situation than us, right now! I mean we could still have each other. I mean I still love you like I did and, you still love me . . . like you did. We could make this work you know, we could . . .

FLO: Richard!

RICHARD: . . . make . . .

FLO: Richard!

RICHARD *(surprised tone):* What?

FLO: You said us . . . we! *(Smiles)*

RICHARD: I did? *(Pause. Realizes)* I did! Yes, I did! *(Laughs)*

They hug each other

RICHARD: But you have to tell me what I didn't understand.

Flo pulls away

RICHARD: Just kidding dear! Just kidding. Come here. *(Pulling her back)*

No thunder sounds
Only a black-out

SCENE—8:

Center Stage—Yoshi, Mariko, and Yuri

Side Stage (L)—Sagar and Ms. Thapa

SAGAR: I don't want to lose my arms, mumma, I don't want to lose my . . . *(Cries)*
MS. THAPA: No! I won't let you lose your arms! There must be a way out of this. *(Springs up)* There has to be another option! Yes! Yes! There must be!

Sagar and Ms. Thapa go into a freeze mode
Yoshi, Mariko, and Yuri see what they are going through

YURI: See, papa! That boy will be losing both his arms. He won't get them back. But you can. We can get back what we have lost.

MARIKO: Yuri's right Yoshi! We'll start afresh, alright. Together.

Pause
Yoshi slowly lowers his arms and lets the knife fall from his hand
He starts to cry and falls down to his knees

YOSHI: I'm sorry! I'm so . . . so . . . sorry. *(Cries)*

Mariko and Yuri quickly run to him
Mariko kicks the knife away; both of them hug him tightly

YURI: It'll be alright papa.
MARIKO: Yes Yoshi, it will.

Sobbing
After sometime the crying fades away

YOSHI: we'll start again. Afresh, together. *(All in a low tone)*

No thunder sounds
Only a black-out

<u>SCENE—9:</u>

Center Stage—Sagar and Ms. Thapa

Side Stage (L)—Richard and Flo

FLO *(shouts):* STOP! STOP! *(Decibel dropped)* Stop! That's it! I mean *(Decibel raised)* THAT'S IT!

RICHARD *(frustrated):* What THAT'S IT DAMN IT!

Argument

FLO *(shouts):* I'M LEAVING! I'M LEAVING, YOU! YOU HEAR ME! I'M LEAVING . . . YOU!

Richard and Flo go into a freeze mode Sagar and Ms. Thapa see what they are going through

SAGAR: Mumma, look! They're about to lose themselves. What could be more painful than that!

His mum looks at him and caresses his arms

SAGAR: I'll live with it mumma! It's just a physical part of me that I'll be losing. My spirit . . . will still be the same. And I have you too, don't' I?

MS. THAPA: Yes! You do . . . my son. My brave . . . son. You do.

She hugs her son
Sagar wriggles his head on her shoulders

SAGAR: I love you mumma.
MS. THAPA: I love you too, son. I love you too.

No thunder sounds, no black-out
The lights fade away, and a song plays
The song—"Life's a Long Song" by Jethro Tull

GLOSSARY

Amar	Immortal
Bhagawan	Divine, godly
Chora	Son
Danava	Demon, evil spirit
Divya shakti	Divine energy or power
Hai	Isn't it?
Makhamali	A flower that does not wither
Marg	Pathway
Nritya	Dance
Om	Mystical and sacred Sanskrit sound
Padmasana	Lotus posture for meditation
Pranaam	To greet with respect
Swami	Who is one with his self
Tapasya	Deep meditation
Tathastu	So be it
Yaar	Friend